THE GREAT
MINDIFICENT

Cesar Tejeda

Copyright © 2024 Cesar Tejeda All Rights Reserved

LCCN: *2024946863*

Contents

Introduction: ii

Chapter One: Let's Paint Together 1

Chapter Two: Who Are You? 20

Chapter Three: GUERITO OJOS De CHICHARO 38

Chapter Four: Pops "I Run the Show" 51

Chapter Five: GEO "High in this" 61

Chapter Six: Who am I "The Opening" 79

Chapter Seven: Risky Business "Play It Safe" 98

Chapter Eight: Gordo the Giant
"for me, everything is easy" 115

Chapter Nine: I'm not a Giant, I'm a God 146

Book Letter 158

Introduction:

I, too, suffered but remained persistent to understand the purpose of my suffering. Growth motivated me to continue even when giving up was an option. I learned to be a student of life so that I could become a teacher for the lost. If you are lost, I wrote this for you. If you want to grow, this is also for you. For those who think they cannot learn, this is especially for you.

Before this, I always stood on the cliff of the abyss, knowing who I was and hiding in my comfort zone, not needing to expose the nature of what I could be until one day, I let go. I learned about peace after knowing about war. I want to tell you the story of my war. I want to show you how to develop your soul through battling your enemies. Enemies are those that oppose your true nature, not always are those in the form of a being, because enemies can be emotions as well. I would say we are all emotional. Some say they have no emotions, but isn't that a feeling itself?

There was a time when I felt nothing, no cares in the world, and was just ready to let it all go to an end. I was sitting on an abandoned bridge on top of the busiest freeway just crying. There was nothing holding me back, no one knew how to find me. I stared at my phone as my sister called relentlessly, she is the person in my life that I would not lie to. I cried harder, thinking of how much pain I was going to cause her, so I turned the phone off. I took a few deep breaths before ending my life when, at the end of the bridge, my name was called out!

It was Chito, a friend that would end up becoming my best friend. I ran to him like a child does to their parents. We collided into a hug filled with my sobbing. I let it all go in his arms, I do not recall the exchange of words, but I could never forget the emotions I felt when I claimed I had nothing left to feel. "I got you," said his hug. "I'm ok," said my soul as I collapsed.

By no means do I promote the ending of a life, this is a serious story of real thoughts. To have no one and then all at once have a person make you feel you have all that you need is as real as life gets. What if you could find all you need inside yourself, would you look? Trust me, I can show you. I trust that I'm a good human and that what I do with the results of my work will be for good and not for evil.

I can honestly say I did my best to leave you alone and not expose you to the things I realized. I wrote about how I feel before making myself vulnerable to your screen shots and judgment. Open your mind and imagine that you're so good at understanding that you can literally be so empathetic to see life through me. I don't think we are just some characters confused amongst one being; I know I am floating freely in others as I found to be in me. I have a deep love for life and an intense admiration for human capacity.

I didn't want to be like a religion where there is hella truth and purity but at the end there's a hook to benefit one single individual. I saw all religions to have one common universal message in which I agree but I saw how man corrupted for their own selfish gain. I took from all and created for the greatness and good of us all, on how we can govern ourselves. If you knew all the shit I forgot, you'd be the smartest person alive, so instead I chose to let you into my head to scan, explore, and see for yourself.

You will attempt to measure my worth but I'm a legend in my own mind. The driving force of my writings is the constant reminder of me being alive, embracing what life freely gives, positive or negative, so that I may share my wit in a service for those afraid to live. It is the wit that uncovered the lies told by those dishonest.

I am the tree, rooted in the soil of our memories, as we stretch our arms to reach a grasp of why we are the way we are. This whole idea was never too much for me. I didn't search for connection, I knew what I was, and I have always been one with nature, connected. This life force was in me and where we all belong.

I could never put myself above you. My greatness didn't translate to such language; I've simply decided to experience it fully throughout my life. It didn't make me the best. This just meant that I would let myself be the being I was always meant to be for us all. The importance isn't about what is, the importance is the connection to what is and the reality of this is easily missed.

Sometimes, you cannot remember your dreams because you must know how to play the right cards at the right moment. This will trigger the keys and doors for them to connect, and only this way will it reveal itself for you without any fog. Be aware that regardless of your intuition, there is no wise move without hidden dangers.

So, what are you impatient for?

It took me seven years to produce this book. I went through every emotion in existence to express my story. The story hasn't even ended, this is the foundation for the basis of my future. I am merely an example of what not quitting can be like for anyone, you too can have a life filled with stories of the events you choose to produce. That's the beauty, everything is a choice. Choices can change your life.

Chapter One:
Let's Paint Together

All my intentions are with purpose and constructed with the support of knowledge gathered through an extensive frequency. A long lifeline, an old soul within this flesh that felt beyond emotional boundaries. Thanks to that, I now constantly feel the shakies. No anxiety, Parkinson's disease, or ADHD. No condition exists in me aside from true experiences from genuine emotions, and everything I feel is certain without a doubt.

My spirit radiates an explosive fire of energy that wakens my whole being. Retained inside in my own silence, I seem timid about exposing who I am. This is because being vocal makes me vulnerable to the filth of your intoxicated understanding. I don't care to be understood, and I won't allow another uneducated mind to determine my needs for medication. I'm comfortable with the five entities in me, no more or less crazy than anyone else, am I? I got it all under control. You'll meet them later; I call them the Me's.

The Me's are all the different versions of myself. They each have their own story, and they all demand to lead the novel. I sometimes call them WE, US or they are also known as The Committee, a branch of decision making that discusses what is best for me. I don't expect you to agree or understand why at times, I do fucked up shit that you feel the need to judge me. We don't like being questioned, so we just consume and let time do what it does best: unravel. The common eye sees me as a single being, so we understand why they don't comprehend.

So, do you really think I'm crazy or is being blind to depth the crazy part? Yes, the wholesome character overrules all core of who one really is, but there can be many underneath the mind. All we want is to bring forth the biggest storm, revealing the course of natural destruction. This disaster leads to self-rehabilitation, showing us countless times the center of peace.

Aside from peace, we also want love. All love meets in the middle, we are allowed to love freely even if maliciously it is for the sake of our own peace and thus should be excused. You call this happy; some get happy in their evil and others in their good. Whatever makes you happy concludes with your peace and allows you to love.

The day that Chito saved me changed my whole life. I had nothing and he gave me everything. He had a spare room at home, more than enough space but most importantly, trust. This was a two-story home 4 bedrooms, 3 bathrooms. Every video game in existence and all the weed we can possibly smoke. Chito is like a little boy in a man's body. He spends most of his time playing video games, and he's really good at it. I would get super stoned and watch him and calculate the way he was going to move around a map, this is how I distracted my mind from all the garbage thoughts I had piled on my soul.

The spare room he gave me I call "The Dungeon," God, I have so many memories battling my demons in that room. Each time I set foot in it, I could hear the screams of all my defeated rivals, victims to my conjuring. I hear praise from the Gods the way a Gladiator heard cheers from the coliseums. In this room, I spent almost two years getting myself together. It begun by facing reality and I quit making pity excuses for my actions and results. In this room, I imagined my new life, a future worth living.

Losing the ignorance of my own bias was the best and worst decision made collectively. This wasn't realized until the decision was already made. I forgave but never forgot, my history was beautiful in all its righteous ways. We didn't hold a single moment in selfishness and in seeking the truth of all beliefs and this was the way ONE whole was created. Never entertained nor distracted, observing soaking in like a sponge. I'm a traveler of lifetimes, cultures, religions, professions, and lifestyles. Many parts of me are unsatisfied and undistinguished from my real needs. An evolving person such as myself shouldn't be left unattended, it's easy to create a swirl of misleading thoughts that may keep you lost in your vision.

In many moments I strayed attempting to give up, and not to forget the countless times the world fucked me and even had me questioning a higher power. I continued blaming circumstances until the day came that I changed myself instead. The road to true happiness was within helping myself, the love for me. I just want to help others avoid unnecessary pain. I want you to find fulfilling love in everything and everyone. You should see all the things you can imagine come together as a painting that you yourself create. Creation is like stuffing yourself with life.

Well, I stuffed myself. I am full of all the knowledge, experience, pains, and joys that living has to offer. I walked so many bridges, meeting statuses that would never blend. Learning so much about many worlds that would never end. That may honestly not even collide.

We are meant to interact with one another. I enjoy attempting to live life through you. Envisioning your ideas by watching how you move. Wishing I could understand you, hoping someday I can live a life that fits your shoes. I would willingly relive my own life until I get it right, all this to prove I'm now here for you and not for me. I'm unselfish, as I can be yet unknown about this place where greed determines if you have more than me.

To make sense of such standards is difficult because although alone, I find myself in need to share. To remind everyone that I don't want to be alone, that life is much better when its shared. That willingly I share the craving for a touch that was once present in me but to always be skeptical of the new reaction. I became weary of what connections I should make.

So, I made sure not to react as I spent time waiting for the usual electricity or energy, if I even make sense. I'm aware that reliving twice what only happens once is unrealistic. Appealing or not, I yearned to inflame my astonishment. My sense of understanding overpowers all attempts to interrupt my comprehension. It has always been my own vibe first, during, and last…. I linger in my own space, and nothing is to invade who I am. I'm a being who learns from all spectrums.

My eyes aren't just a physical tool they're very much aware of the unknown, having visibility that doesn't require sight. The hearing detects vibrations, there's flow in rhythms and believe they mean something that words can't express. Fragrance meshes and confuses many with the notion that they can't smell, where I marinate to distinguish the origin and separate them as individuals. I'm that person who savors a moment without over consuming. When and lucky, if there's ever contact know I'm exchanging a part of me for your most valuable asset. Energy, I want it, it belongs to me. I use all this to relive, imagining the engraved tunes of my past life's bringing the music I conduct. I'm a creator, so don't insult me in disbelief.

I don't believe in Gods, I AM GOD…well, a piece of that infinite essence. God is in everything and everyone. I've always believed in that. I believe in everything, the endless possibilities of good and evil. The hopeless casualties that conform and give up dreaming, I did everything for you. My contagious vision full of joyful sorrow is a distinctive way to live. At this point I have somewhat broken free from the bullshit Matrix that likes to loop in repetition. I couldn't allow living to limit who I am. Now it's time to help everyone else make their dreams come true showing you who you are inside and not this superficial ad you continue recreating to attempt and fit in somewhere…. Anywhere.

Let's show you a Universal equation for when you feel lost, unloved, or confused so that you can find your way home. The place where you come to peace with even the filthiest actions. Don't dare say you don't have a home because I've opened my doors and windows just so you can be sure that you are welcome. We are all crazy and we all want to find a way to cope or understand.

Shit, some of us just want to live another day and know we are making the right decisions. Let's forgive and never forget that it all makes us who we are. This forgiveness is only found in the darkest dungeons of torture, left completely alone in what seems like eternity. This is what within looks like. Be fully self-involved where your cries for help echo in solitude, imagining what you knew before all this as the only thing keeping you alive.

Engraved tunes expose a lunatic conduction before self-destruction. Go through a suppression that will be fooling you with a mirage of doubts because you don't get exactly what you want how you want. Our vision is never about the scenery or resources nor what we are going through. Although acknowledging that it's a secondary factor to the background which helps you understand, your direct interactions allow you to follow up.

This is all a true mind fuck but so simple to take in your own version of how it should be and when you have that answer just know that's exactly what it is. Just your answer. Learn from a crazy guy, only then will my soul tare off its last bit of flesh left from the simulation we live in and float into the infinity.

Infinity is the end of this life and the beginning of the next, where one fully stabilizes their self being into a freedom that society doesn't allow for the sake of control. It's just childish greed that also came to understand infinity but instead of helping, they decided to use our time diverting into temptations of false hope. Telling us what to believe, what to want, and what your needs are. Molding you behind your sockets. Teaching barriers and counter urge to disrupt purity with confusion and a waste of time. Make a choice, knowing the fine print and that you can live with it but proceed in evolving your genuine self.

To do so, search for you, race at your fastest pace. Master your own mind by indulging in your every moment. Feel all aspects of all your senses. Taking in as much time to really get to know yourself not what your parents, media, society, Gods tell you to know. What do you feel? This is all done at your own pace, it's

YOUR race and never forget it's all about YOU. I see in you what I see in me.

The fine print states,

"Everything is on the line, keep in mind the heavy price of hurting all you love to love many more."

I learned to be selfish regardless of how badly you perceived me. I forgive you because I know it was difficult for you to see the value of what I was meant to do. You had no idea who I was born to be. The end goal of my true happiness was that all I loved someday would result in the reciprocation of the love I felt I had earned. Unconditional love is always willing of the worst products, this is the kind of love everyone seeks. Love me for me. Love me with all my powers. Care for me in all my weaknesses. I wanted to receive, so I stopped giving it away. I only gave forth.

In life, there's a filter; all those who fade away only want to use you, and the rest are willing to be used. This doesn't make one a bad person, remember I mean GOOD in my story. Stay aware that those who stick around must want or get something in exchange, even if your contribution is as simple as that of a company. At the end of the day, you still gave back, except in this thinking, there's no need to sacrifice yourself and you still please those pleasing you. This is a beautiful exchange of energy. Everyone wins without a petty speculation of doubt. These are the Laws of Balance.

Laws are created to put order in areas that need to be guided. To place a system of regulating whatever is determined to be acceptable. There's no such thing as good or bad; it's all just vocabulary used to communicate our own feelings. I had to stop feeling for others, sympathy is still a feeling of my own anyway. So technically, we never honestly feel for others. I could feel hot or cold around anyone, it is either I'm in tuned, or it's FUCK YOU.

Living for me and this makes you irrelevant as you are pointing your little finger, trying to judge me and not having the slightest might to fight the fight that I took on. I took on the responsibility that no one else had the will to do so. It was easy to blame the odds of life, to say that I was insignificant. This was not the case for me; I had a battle within that was worth the attention of the universe.

I sat back and observed the cleansing of souls squirming swiftly away from me, scattering like a whirlpool of chaos. I felt the destruction in my core. Death was the only thing left here, a desert of decaying skulls fogged in the dust left by bone residue and skin flakes cycling the atmosphere forever. I was departing from the third dimension, experiencing your same reality although perceiving with a different manner.

Physically, I remained rooted while accepting an invisible awareness. My 3D time was spent speeding as I was discovering the loopholes on the run. Literally, I have always been on the run. I was chased by society's standards of who I "had" to be and what I needed to do for others. This was extremely ignorant, coming from lost and uncertain circumstances. I suppose that, at its time, it served its purpose as a part of the growing process.

Change is how one grows; to some, this may be more uncomfortable than others. Attempt not to give that idea too much thought and just take on the challenges. Challenges led me to many failures but in those disappointments, I recovered to see new light. This new place I found is lonely, and just how darkness overwhelms your vision, so does the light.

Imagine that we are in a system playing a game that requires one to pass levels to get ahead and experience a change. Something new, different from everything you already know. When you quit, that becomes your own limit; if you ever plan to finish this game of life, there's no other way but to pick up where you left off. My mind has come up with various ideas from which I have yet to come to a conclusion. The most entertaining one is how many times have I actually lived?

Déjà vu is this bottling unexplained form of you existing in a past memory, like overlapping a moment you once lived with a new chance to make a different choice and redirect where you left off. That's what happened to me every time I let go of a job, jumping from home to street to home repeat. Leaving connections scattered in my belongings, the aura of my energy lingering in all that which made contact with me.

Can you be a multidimensional soul in many different places at once? Yup, we have the ability to tune into our own wavelengths regardless of how far. If you know a place or feeling you visited in the past, focus and go back anytime you want. All my own realities move in awareness, bilocating at my own thoughts. Thinking is important but through confusion, you only advise perceptions that lead to emotions, and you won't succeed in mastering your self-enemy.

So, I feed on the connections from even this new solitude. It's my mind vs myself and I win every time. This is what a real vampire is like, draining everything I had once left behind and feeding on its history. It made me infinite. I'm not this fanged super speed human who only comes out at night. I'm a real person who acquires energy from my past, present, and future.

Conscious of how I was draining others, you must know I'm well aware of my new level. Just like playing Super Mario after you beat the level but go back to pick up the coins you passed up or missed. I need all of me, all that is for me. There's absolutely no way that I can take from this world at no cost. My whole life, I've been more than willing to pay. A war at my fingertips and the world on my palm.

Entering a war zone but I know what I'm dealing with. I know energy can't be created or destroyed, resulting in the confidence that I could see everything through eventually, just like in past levels. Anything can become a dead end if you allow it to, or you can pick up where you left off and see it through. I'm going to see this through for sure.

It was when I finally knew better, I did better. I started working, endlessly spending every living second on the idea that I was more than an empty vessel. That God had a plan to use me as a tool for all his work. With all this power, nothing could stop me now.

Obstacles became irrelevant in the understanding that quitting is the only way you lose. How could I let a wall stop me if hammers and C4 exist? I have all the resources to change my old, boring life. I would find a way to use the systems that were already in place to work for me not I for them. Financial cages were once a problem for me, it takes money to make money, and to make my dreams happen, a 9 to 5 wasn't going to make shit happen.

"Money is solely for the sake of something else… It's not the answer, just the motive."

I, we… It doesn't really matter and there's zero care as to how anyone refers to us, saying I is easier for you to understand who we are. I feel like there are multiple versions of who I am in a single life. There are many voices in my mind trying to make decisions all at once. I've mastered the way I think, so when you face me, you won't be able to see the discussion happening in my thoughts.

Too much had been sacrificed to share my story with you and to beat this game. I sat alone too many times, reminiscing all the emotions I've endured. I paced through space, blurred vision from the tears of joy and pain but all blessings nonetheless. The lessons of life disguised for my unraveling. Joy and pain are an equal force regardless of the definition and I was never fooled to separate their equality.

Crying or laughing, the knowing of my awakening was present, even more so as time progressed. I felt elevation advancing, so I drowned in all my senses to ensure I lived every moment completely mindful. If any similar emotions came back around, I would have a better opportunity of coping and understanding before I lost my mind. To struggle was acceptable but quitting wasn't.

You wouldn't believe how many times I pulled myself out from quitting. I was polished by friction, no being can walk this life without shit happening. I sat in front of a mirror to talk to myself, and it was during this time that I met God. I was on a bender in Las Vegas. I was ready to quit and although I was so high beyond regular limits somehow, I was conscious. I went into a jacuzzi with the pool safe buoy wrapped around my chest. I knew I would drown without it.

I'm a great swimmer but imagine being so high you can't feel anything other than great. Think of what you would do if you send your body commands and it's irresponsive. All I was thinking is that there's no better way to die than being this high. Life was crap, nothing was good enough, and all my thoughts were negative. My mind was weak, and my soul was dying. I was so lost.

When I was floating, I could hear voices asking if I was okay. No one could save me, they were just as high as I was. At this moment, I realized it was time to get out. Physically, there was a group of friends there too, but I was truly alone. We made It back to the house, where we racked more lines to snort. I leaned over for a line but placed my hand on the wall for support and the whole room changed.

Why was I in the jungle? I could see plants all around me, the soil hugging my feet as I moved back. I was definitely not in control and I was confused. My back bumped into another wall and the room tumbled into another change. The ocean right in front of me? I could hear the waves crashing on the shore as the faces blurred and disappeared. I had to get myself together.

I went to the bathroom to wash my face, hoping that would help. The water spilled like all the lies I had told myself throughout my entire life. I was wearing a seamless mask of a kitten's face vomiting rainbows and when I looked up, it smiled at me. I jumped back, cautious of what I was seeing.

He decided to have a conversation:

He- "You're scared of me"

Me- "No, I'm not scared of anything"

He- "You're fake"

I responded, "You're not real, none of this is real."

I knew I was super high. This wasn't even close to over. The reflection in that mirror was the truest version of myself. The conversation with myself continued, I conclude that my whole life had been a lie. Not being able to be honest with myself and constantly trying to make others happy.

My reflection taught me that I needed to have self-love. That God is that single honest part inside of you. The purest form of honesty that we can perform. It was so crazy the way I disconnected to find myself, I felt it strange that one could be so lost yet have so much opportunity. I understand that this really is not over until it's over.

Losing your mind dismisses any attachment to the belief in life itself. There's no correlation between the purpose of life and your own being. Progress is a loop and walls crush you in attempts to cease answers to questions about who you could become. I got tired and let go a couple different times. Getting lost floating away was intriguing at first, since when was it possible to see flavors or taste sound? How could I go from world to world?

Another door to life I opened. Each door I opened had coins to collect, knowledge, I mean, it's the same thing to me: coins and knowledge. Once again, I left a trail of my energy in the spaces I traveled to. God the mind is an extraordinary instrument, difficult to tame but worth the headache for its power. Each mind injects constant frequencies with every thought we put out into the Universe. All with the depth of manifesting realities out of pure energy.

Thoughts have the power to change the course of life. This can be positive or negative. What I do know is we get to do with it what we want. I've made myself purposely sad, running directly towards the hurricanes of misery of my past. For example, my most common storm is the one of my father's absences and then comparing that to how I've missed parts of my own children's memories, knowing the exact pain.

I always start shaking in desperation, seeing no end to the storm of my own choices. I know that life keeps going, that time is constant with no pause moments. I myself chose to let everything go at times. Abandoning gravity in the consumption of suffering, I loved these moments too, puncturing my heart while it's hiding under rocks. Diving deeper into the judgmental ideas of others. I can hear the voices talking shit, they want to put me down.

They are trying to dim my light. After all, I went through to become the "lunatic" I am. You can't imagine the timeless investment I exchanged for the lack of faith. Everything I did to get these answers became a gap of distortion to my connections. Thanks for all the doubts, they kept me pushing when things got tough.

The same kind of voices which are unaware of any background knowledge, chemical balance, spirituality, or the energy each person wants to transcend to their highest power. This is aside from all the labels, religions, and ethnicity possibilities, which can be endless. We must peak in life to be fully pleased, no matter the topic. How ignorant is for anyone to assume authority or opinion over another?

Why not all just seek happiness within their own space, start accepting that each individual is one and only. Let's not set up our own tragedies of disappointments by resenting things we can't control. Instead let's learn from all surroundings and not make this over judging our imperfections.

Admitting negativity to a world sinking into depression has never been my thing. I am what I stand for, a solid nurturing transmitter that can't be contained. The light that connects to the dark side, a true balance for peace. Peace is my happy place, the peak that pleases me most. When I'm not content, I can't rejoice in mediocre joyful moments, they just aren't enough. They don't feel as good without the deep exhale of letting go. I want to live more and tell you more.

Life is full of options, and those who get stuck to their choices will be permanently bonded with regret for not finding peace that shows them transparent happiness. Don't get lost in a *what if* or *what is* not. Chase the peace and happiness you'll find. With this same focal point, I practiced creating positive results at the center of my thoughts so that the words I spoke drew others to me.

When I saw them hearing with their attention signaled I had them trapped, I taught them how to laugh until they smiled, exposing the four chemicals they forgot. Dopamine is the blood pressure support that flows through our system, sending messages between our nerves. My favorite is Oxytocin, the hormonal love drug that strengthens empathy, trust, sexual activity, and our relationship-building. The one you drain most is Serotonin, the key hormone in charge of stabilizing our mood, impacting the whole body and connecting the brain to our nerves. Final but not least are Endorphins to relieve stress and pain like a natural opioid that natural high euphoria.

I stand firm to again state, "I DON'T NEED DRUGS." I understand myself and I don't need any help other than the laws of science and my intuition. I used all my grasp of awareness in order to manipulate future outcomes and success started to surface. It was when I stopped wanting the world, that the world began to want me.

The best laws are those of attraction because they make one feel valued. There is a difference between love and possessing someone. Possessing is the complete opposite, and it took me many failed attempts to understand this. I wasn't possessive; on the contrary, I believed in freedom. It is in freedom that true love will always make its way back to you. To be free was the foundation of my thoughts on the things I wanted. I spoke out loud about a partner who would let me guide and trust my insanity.

I am not perfect in any way, my being and structure can change at any moment, depending on the circumstances. Even so, I had the idea to create a team like no other with little players filled with her love and my brains. There was a long road of success that needed to materialize first but this was my motivation to get past the lonely days. Should this reality reach my possession, I swore to give my life to them.

I focused on the realms of my mind to bring in the tangible. I did this by practicing the functions of the brain and how it connected with the spiritual aspects of the unknown universe. There's no right way to understand yourself and this world, so I tried everything. It's hard to determine what created success within me. Nothing was easy and I failed many times to finally be tired enough to stop fucking around and put in the work I was destined to do.

You would think no one would be able to deal with my inconsistencies from the constant hunt for new evolving ideas. I would be lying if I said I did all this on my own. There is a handful of people who crossed my life amongst my travels. They lent me hands to help me get up when I fell, and ears to listen to my stories to assure they were worth telling. I am forever grateful for them, even for the ones that didn't stick it out. Most importantly, it was God that carried me when I collapsed and fell with no energy to continue. Thank you for never letting me give up on myself and letting me find my way.

I want you to watch the birth of creation, admire the manifestation with your own eyes and witness my true power. Make sure not to blink during this extensive journey and enjoy it as much as you will at the ending. I didn't just ask for things; I commanded the Universe to slave to my words. There was a feeling of power descending upon me from all the time spent investing in repetitive thoughts. I was resilient for never giving up on my dreams, I stood high above life as a giant in this little world. Always honest with my wants and needs, reminding everyone to mind their business and let me be me.

Let me remind everyone to always be themselves to chase their dreams. To believe in those unrealistic thoughts that linger in the back of their mind. Don't listen to anyone who doesn't support because the day you make it happen, it'll be those same people who will eat their words. I believe in you the same way I always believed in me. If you ever feel like giving up, trust in me to carry you.

The only truth to our own perceptions is the feelings that follow our senses. This still, is our own sense even if inaccurate to others. Each unique and inside there is a frequency, a spark in the energy we create that make our heart beats. Life taught me when I decided to learn. I watched, I listened, I felt, I tasted, and I smelled. Most importantly, I paid attention to those senses.

Staying in tune to secure command on which sense needs to be shut off by desensitizing which emotions to feel and at what time to feel. Controlling my whole being and when to release the currents that cause feelings. The feeling is all that makes me human; other than that, I belong to a different universe. Right here right now, with everything tangible, I kept in mind that reality was only a matter of perception. Words are a naïve form of communication filled with assumptions and barriers to failure.

Vocabulary differs in terms of the versatility of views, morals, experiences, etc. Rich could refer to One million dollars and be so life changing while other wealth is in knowledge. I've experienced both countless times, rich and poor, in both spectrums. Money has positive and negative outcomes just like knowledge. I sold drugs and made 30k per day for 4 years straight, and I did drugs and slept at the park while I couch surfed. As my knowledge grew, so did understanding. The truth is that once I understood, it made it much more difficult to coexist with those who have yet ventured away from their innocence.

Letting life do and undo with me as it pleased me as the spectator of my own journey. I lived here in your world peacefully secluded. Draining all my soul connections and allowing the rebel out of the cage to feed, knowing he was a devil to tame. My thoughts being the leash of certain control. I felt that same control was achieved by other Mes, allowing them to dictate the extent reached without losing sight of who I was all in one.

I am a man of peace and love. Holding the leash firm, four against one, all arguing for command, unaware of the notes I took over their views so that I could direct them in one sense. Although we all conflict, I allow freedom for how vital we are to each other's wholesome existence. Been learning from myself my entire life, all inner Mes meshing in preparation for the outer world. What would I allow anyone to assume of me, knowing it's I who paints the image they obtain?

Chapter Two:
Who Are You?

At this point, I am younger than I believe, but I already have the master key in my possession. I was well aware that a lot of life awaited me, yet I couldn't unlock the door that held me back from success. I questioned things that one shouldn't, like if God was not with me or a part of me as I thought? Was I regular, the predictable cliché to give up now and conform after all the investments? To not live up to my destiny and be Great was unacceptable.

I lacked the information to process a full understanding of why I was failing. It was as if when I was barely getting up, life would slam me down again. Humbling my stubbornness, teaching me to be grateful. This reminded me that I didn't know it all and that my failures came from that same weakness. To think I was absolute perfection made me weak. When I was truly meant to be strong, strong minds can endure the burden that people run from. For me, each time, it became easier getting up and trying again.

Life made it clear to me that we all have highs and lows. A life of peace is unlikely given, this is a life one must create. It will be difficult attempting to find your true self and you will be exhausted with the need for serenity. To quiet down the noise is not an easy task to conquer. I traveled many worlds to figure me out and many more to figure us out. Searching before, during, and after for anything I could have ever missed.

I've been lost in the chromatic shadows of life, taking the time and admiring as I saw the black spread on the white, creating greys. Who would have thought that one can feel vibrant within so much plain color. The colors inconsistently faded within mortality, creating a high so twisted that it felt like everything was black. It's the darkness that chases us, but I had no fear. I started hunting purposefully with the intention to be bigger than my mistakes and tribulations.

In this war, many times, I thought it was over. This is the illusion of my sanity, for everything to end and find peace. I had to forgive myself when I made mistakes and just try to be better. It's unrealistic to surmise that I am better. That I changed many times and just got better. That from a person like me you can solely receive positivity.

It's a real choice to be positive or negative. To command your very own thoughts and disguise the nature of your own actions and emotions is also a choice. I don't believe lies, so I follow laws. Laws that guide me to create the right life. I like the idea of laws being a fact and some sort of real proof to this mind fuck we battle while living.

My battle has always been in my mind. There's an immense list of problems and solutions I plan to make decisions on. There is a longer list of things that I'm not even prepared to live. I stress that I understand that this is a hard life, but it truly is a beautiful one. I made my way to understanding life by its laws.

It's a law that any force creates an equal or opposite force. I noted, "this was law" each time I leveled up. It's inescapable to hit rock bottom before the bounce up. The outcome would result in equal opposing energy depending on how hard I collided into pieces. We should accept this without an argument. Once agreed upon, a new level emerges, it's that simple to pass any level just accept it and what it comes with so that you may move forward.

Let me tell you about life and what it was like for me when I began to understand. The growth was exponential, with nothing to hold me back. Knowledge was instilling a fuck it in my system slowly but surely. Almost instantly, the mind settles down when you don't allow the voices of others to judge who you are. You wouldn't care to understand the extent of my needs for stability; I just want to be content.

It was within these needs that I created the faith of endless realities and possibilities. I dragged myself all over the world, attempting to maintain a grip of my own judgement. I did all this just to form a genuine identity of who I wanted to be. It wasn't easy, it was a drag.

I never liked it easy in my whole existence. And if the drag wasn't enough, I would puddle and walk. Have you ever heard the term puddle walking? It's when you're all loopy and high off drugs and the floor feels like water. Your knees are weak with no real power to remain up. This is what a majority of life had been like for me. Difficult to stay up. Looking at me, you could never tell, some would say I had it easy.

You couldn't tell that I was lost in the sauce, being faithful to my true confusion as the questioning would continue forever. I was always tumbling in the currents of life in search of a stable place that would provide love, peace, and support. I had no clue that the truth was all about me. I made it my life goal to create this place of love, peace, and support so I could teach others how to do the same.

Essentially, I knew nothing of myself, so I could really start anywhere. My foundation was iffy because of the lack of answers my past truly gave me. I knew religions, but none convinced me to commit fully. I wanted answers that had no doubts to satisfy my understanding. It was because of this that I decided to work on my spirit. I knew that regardless of religion, my soul spoke to me from within.

To build a healthy consciousness, I made myself aware of my own faults. I forgave myself and wrote down each time I felt I could have done better. The idea was to align my thoughts to a certain action that would transform me into the best version of myself. To learn what I needed to do in order to control my chi. Deciding when to contain and when to release, manipulating the outcomes of my very own life. The thought of my own mind control dictating the possibilities and results of my story is a movie.

I began to change in even the simplest forms. Eating healthier made me feel better, and I stayed away from the bad influences that would fog my vision. I physically kept busy with any form possible, putting pressure on my temple. I even avoided social media and television, not preoccupied, or allowing time to pass by while I remained stuck in space.

Instead, I learned to advance, working on me only so that someday I could serve others. Soon enough, the wait was over and peering like a commoner was also over. Taking advantage of the enlightenment that was presented upon my path. Humbly bowing down to the inner God who ran all of the Me's. Just imagine perfecting various versions of yourself who play in different worlds. In each and every world, you are Great.

He was GREAT! Acknowledging the knowledge that I was to be infinite. Always seek guidance from the universe by reaching out to connect because the battle is never alone. My light, my dark, my life and together we vibe. Realizing I truly never was alone, everything is here without a need to label it. IT'S ALL HERE! The good, bad and all that's in between.

You see I felt the lengths our senses can go. I did this so that I would grow to appreciate the fact that all life was one feel to action away. Outcomes varied but ultimately, the choice made was exactly what I decided and wanted. Heaven and Hell creating my Universe, the mesh infinite of delusions for illusions… Helixion. A repeating cycle where one point meets itself, enforced by positive and negative outcomes. I pieced that together, you need to take notes; I don't make shit up that has no meaning.

This idea of infinity had an infraction, if infinity was real, how so? What about heaven or hell? Or was I in a simulation? I had a theory, a really good one. Consciously, I am alive and in existence, although I wonder gradually while living. Energy keeps my vessel alive, maintaining the function of my organs. Energy can't be created or destroyed, but my vessel can. This body can end, supposably releasing my energy to fill a new space. Like when a light bulb breaks, the energy it once stored finds a gap to fill like a radio or tv. I'm asking myself repeatedly, "Energy can't be created or destroyed?"

Everything is a source of energy; positive, negative, or neutral. None defined good or bad but are all powers within one whole. The entire Universe is a massive idea of tiny little specs creating life. We all break down to 99.9% atoms, the smallest constituent part of all life's elements. Undermined and dismissed are the small atoms that create us are miniature vortices of energy that remain active even when separated. I think that even if the vessel "dies" we remain alive, simply in pieces. Basically, each atom vortices exhibiting its own energy personality, vibrating at its own frequency. Being itself.

Regardless, the microscopic size of an atom is technically physical… 99.9% physical. That .1% missing, I believe, is God, the soul and spirit form that we can't physically see in "our imagination." In all religions, I have studied, God is "EVERYWHERE", but they can't explain something justifiable for nonbelievers to agree 100%.

Now let's question that if everything breaks down to 99.9% atoms then the .1% must be God. Therefore, God is in everything so we ourselves are God yet I'm humbly aware that the only God higher is that .1% connected to all. We are merely a common one of 99.9% atom pieces of a whole 100% thus .1% being the single most unmistakable difference within 100%. Call me crazy all you want and find opposing arguments I really don't care because this theory changed me.

I accepted I could be wrong, but I needed those opposing theories to challenge who I am, and I still wouldn't conform to rules and regulations others set for me like I once did before this thinking. I'm not the same as before; I'm lost and confused, and I wouldn't be again. Needing to be told what to do not knowing my true identity. I decided to never conform and instead savor the freedom of being limitless, infinite. God being in me, and I in everything.

I'm grateful to have a place to lay my faith over and the feeling of security at the very least. Believing in myself when I was so lost before. I can't imagine going back to doing what life told me to do without certainty. The choice to my beliefs, wants, and needs were actually my own. I am my own creator in this life, I invest my energy into the God that I am, and I am he. We are one, I forgave myself for all my faults, leaving them behind me to focus on my present lessons and become the best I, in this very moment. That's God's forgiveness. I showed others the steps I had taken in hopes that they would find their way. Don't fight back, if not you'll just glitch, just flow in the current and you will live on.

"Fellow atoms and God, I'm grateful for our force and wavelengths. For we are one, everyone has a piece of me, including your investment in the reality of life."

Investing back, sharing the thoughts on these papers. Sharing the insight created by all of you! The multitude who crossed my path or even the path of those who crossed those who crossed me and so on. It goes on forever! Infinite! Boundless! We are one huge, amazing organism. I'm in tune because I sacrificed my entire life, it wasn't easy. Love, children, career, family, friends, and the safety net of my stability. My whole image so that I'd be able to share my little light with everyone.

You never know when your light can go out, and you'll use me. Don't worry I've forgotten all the times you didn't believe in me and how much I struggled on my own. I hold no grudge I'm still the same crazy you never believed in. I'm actually a real crazy now allowing my own torture for us. I remember everyone saying I was selfish not knowing my great plan of existence.

    Here's the endless love, solid the warrior of souls in the midst of all this confusion and barriers. I gave an offering of eternal repose, a journey hovering above my own flesh. Surrendering any attachment to worries, drifting into an inerrant perfection. This is our destiny and true self. A soul who isn't attached but instead abides to nature's natural ruling. I have no past modified lives in their current moment, working with no control of what the future holds, only controlling their reactions to what comes. I wait reading to react. I see multiple life's happening all at once.

    .1% is solid purity, a reality of the deepest imagination with real conclusion. Fairy's, demons, and edible buildings magically free to intrude our vision. An instant in the distance of what really is real. Everything is. I'm in this game of life forever reincarnating shedding old lives like snakeskin as I'm evolving. Dying over and over, my soul representing the skin to my continuation.

    There is an illusion in my sanity dictated by the complexity of thoughts created to concentrate the mind on practical things since I constantly disappoint those around me, as if my sacrifices weren't enough. Many battles have been lost but the war has always been my victory. It is unreasonable to accept anything less.

    Attempting to contest change is deceiving, a great lie I would never tell. All doubts that are fed compromise the reality of how pure I come. Those are doubts that fabricate pain, disbelief, and misdirection. Every time, I'm already in belief of currents created by this, thinking it's wrong. I'm prepared in the wrong direction, disloyalty sneaking into the heart, already manifesting stress in my perimeter, taking bites of my soul, knowing failure is within what is tainted.

I hurt beyond usual this way, being selfish becomes selfless because getting to know myself first allowed me to understand other perceptions and to accept them. I feel that bringing a story of freedom is important for all. Undressing you and peeling through layers of doubts, one after another. Your soul, fidgeting in anxiety, itching for touch, but you're insecure. The disbelief of a reality picture perfect, ideal to fulfill your every thrill.

Your thoughts sweating overfilled with emotions as your neurons sabotage your chemical balance. Intimately spiraling the conscious government, the natural decisions that incline all surrounding atmosphere. Loves continuous battle where flesh, mind, and soul intertwine in a dance promiscuously teasing with a hypnotic result to perfectly fuck all intuition in existence. Creating a fondness toward what I am that fogs the path of your reality. I'm sorry, that's what love does: manipulating with aggressive behavior. It can be so toxic, so we must remain proactive and avoid weird ideas. Remember that force reciprocates, and it will shoot back the same energy you put out.

Love and hate are one, and I accept and support a balance from both. Refraining from questions because I approve of all ideas and their forms. Madness set me free, and if this hadn't been my choice, I would have always been the type of person to obey. Even within this realm, I made myself separate; I was in disguise, incognito like a telegram, putting everything aside for a clear vision. Tunnel vision conquered my life, only seeing things one way and that was my way.

I studied in silence good substance, productivity keeping me hidden from the masses and unknown to earth's nature. Why play games when I can't benefit from perfidious intentions. Barriers mean nothing to evolution and earning the knowledge exempted me from avoiding blame. No discipline required to obtain my goals, it was all about letting go of societies obligations and I began to put concrete affairs in order with no rules because there is no risk. No leverage over my soul because I kept it that way.

Regardless of what it cost; seeking truth and to make that voice the dominant one is where my salvation resides. With this I would transcend the moral code achieving true emptiness. A mere mirage of what living is. A well-executed plot of existence without clarity nor certainty and yet I knew this is true. A state of consciousness beyond our known dimensions where we find balance. How amateurish to allow one's vibe to determine one's own, I can't because the waves coast at my rhythm. I feel that I experience victories and failures in life alone, conditioning as time progressed, and I do my best with what I must work with to accept my results.

Minding my own business absent of sound, memories always flood my brain while my surroundings speak in the distance. Ordinary life didn't interest me. We are connected to a higher purpose preexistent with immortality. Memories attended the realities that never define me as an altered image. To maintain my focus on growth beyond the basic standard.

As I discovered, I destroyed. No passage in life is safe, all dangerously infect the mind. It was fear that would determine my future. I am my own virus with no safe word. Assuming my life had been lived long before the arrival on this timeline, I wandered into the profundity of the universe, deciphering the nuance of vibrations and many times, I got lost. My grip faded as time passed, by the time I wanted to snap back, my soul had transformed forever and it was here that things became the chaotic collision I relive every day.

Examining the experience rather than living in my emotions brought me to this deserted state of mind that I own. I now roam continuing my quest for life and the purpose I must fulfill. Life's timeclock uninterrupted as I fell out of sync from everything around me. I realized that while deep in myself I was missing the moments that made me an incomplete whole. Not sure if I fell behind or went too far ahead but the notions that came from exploring and experimenting with life costed me everything before I even had it.

The typical life that most find themselves content with was never for me. A good career to maintain a household filled with my children, and a happy wife just wasn't enough to give me a happy life. I could never be fooled into a system that provided a purpose so small that it only made a difference to a single household. I always had dreams of my life meaning to others as much as it meant to me. So, I took the time to understand myself and then introduced myself to the world.

I was away for too long figuring out the world, missing the times I wish were mine with my own family. It was the moment my mind was poisoned with such thought that I detected something even worse than craving death and living dead. It was difficult to accept that I was missing out on so much for myself but that someday, I would be able to pay it forward. Sometimes, I even envied those living their "happy" little life.

Living had many negative moments but I always found lessons with positive results within those moments. Nothing made this new feeling of envy feel better nor go away. Initially, torturing my own mind with thinking of moments I knew had no reliving. Remembering my mission to check my feelings, I couldn't stay worried.

I had no place in my soul to truly envy anyone because deep inside, I wanted all of us to experience that good life. It took a ton of arguments with myself just to stay sane. I heard many voices oppose my beliefs and doubt my methods, but I remained firm on everything I agreed to do.

No one is like me handling opportunities so recklessly. Anything I missed was unaccounted for in the air, I couldn't perceive the feeling to make my own environment. This was also poison. Venom overruling my body to the bone, like acid deterrence slowly becoming another accession to the wonders of the universe. Melancholy was the price for knowledge, surpassing all sorrow I ever knew.

"No one was going to love me."

Those words lingered in corners of all I knew. Believing in me was obviously improbable and concluded in my dubious thought for anyone. Including my own parents as if jumping off a cliff with me, trusting that we would survive was hindering the climax of their love for me. I was alone in my mind, despising the world that I mentally created. It was unrealistic to blame anyone for their doubts because I was crazy in my dreams with a future of perfection.

No one believed in my crazy dream, there was so much knowledge gathered with no physical evidence of success. Everyone questioned when was I going to grow up? "Never," I replied in my mind. I kept all my childish dreams to feed the magic in me. Ideas and concerns of this magnitude are a high of their own, and no one was ready to peak with me forever, so I got high on my own. It was always me against the world, and I had no expectations of anything more.

There was an obsession cycling in my heart, reminding me that to progress, I needed to always be in attendance at any event. My life is an adventure that requires inventing as the unknown unfolded at my feet. To be face to face expecting a flinch, a blink at the very least but got nothing out of me. I would never blink as if I had doubts. I know that everything is for my taking for my creating and for my doing.

Becoming more virtuous than a human itself embarking into a journey filled with life to absorb. A life that most escape by excusing with a day-to-day life. The luxury of remaining in comfort is defined as, "A BITCH". Like why not become your truest self? Why allow the chackles of stability, and the fear to live keep you hostage. Only a coward would avoid risks for progress and settle by playing it safe.

The ancients speak through me as the youth does too. Representing the lengths of my understanding. I have lessons at my fingertips, kneeling to my senses for the leap of faith.

Accepting fluent forces is the ultimate beauty, the reward in itself. I suffered profoundly heart and soul; my own life was my own work. Secluded but I was going UP, evolving mentally an ardent love. I allowed many humans to experience me and take a piece, yet I remained alone. I took from you to learn what not to be and what not to show.

You who witnessed the relentless quest I set for myself, found yourself roaming a vacant purpose with intentions to recondition but still saw nothing. I populated what you covered in vandalism with an exchange of new existence. An opportunity to live a true life. One free of despondency with an extensive sense of preservation in the sanctuary of love where pain deteriorated in evanesce. Ardently supporting dexterous behavior that stimulates the soul into neglecting all physical awareness.

Welcome to a dreamland ride of dreams going around and around reliving every luscious second spent. Our feelings truer than any truth from which they were born. A presence that replenishes all desires. Beyond fairytales, the dreams yearned, unknown the nature our soul hovers above to simply envy what the body can feel. The wind brushing against one's structure, thoughts between bliss and sin invade the soul with rupturing. Filling with an illusion, a truth is the ONLY truth. The remedy, Oh, is so heavenly, where you can't help but remain faithfully vowed from beginning to end to recycle and find once again. The purest you, the God in you.

Regardless, always holding myself to a standard code, not one by the streets nor the books. A code of my own, one that I aired from the life I lived. Still living that life constantly revising and adapting. A truth that paved my way, always staying honest with myself solid to that, bending like a noodle but never breaking. Making it concrete to continue moving, unsure if this was beneficial for my life or if it made so many complications not worth the time and effort.

I was more than one, always thinking for many. For instance, I catch every angle so that the details are endless. I see the gaps people ignore for a bias, attempting to build bridges instead of a road through thinking they'd go unnoticed. As if I were a regular idiot consumed by the critics of society, that I'd be blind in inundation to not see patches under the paint. If anything snuck past my vision, I know that I felt it anyway. My gut always talking to me so I can't ignore anything.

All these years I spent isolated paying attention to my gut, not only what I thought I felt but also verifying if those thoughts and feelings were honest. Working hard, fighting smart, and loving effortlessly. I was in this process as a whole and slowly drifting, breaking down piece by piece until there would be nothing left of me. I felt trampled by life.

It didn't matter because it was all registered in my brain, it was all for me and I owned it. Registering every experience as all of the Me's thought of it, I listened to their opinions as I took into consideration their ideas for one full thought to decide and make words to actions. The fact is I have multiple personalities in the intense state I am, many Me's an odd idea but God is the real crazy one for dealing with all of us and making one mind. The God within overruled the inner Me's, God is I my truest self. The more of the .1% I became, the less of the 99.9% remained being irretrievable to existence.

No longer a foolish man living for myself but instead wise with purpose. Whatever achieved served a higher power with the exchange for eternal life living beyond our lifetimes. I'm a good human, misunderstood from the purest good quality intentions. Bettering myself with moral and intellectual virtue, understanding others became a valuable activity while passing the time.

There wasn't anyone who saw this coming, it was a rooting seed you didn't plant and a life you didn't even know existed. Reviving with knowledge the solitude of soul connection. I am a traveler of lifetimes who read books a school didn't force onto me. I read of those things in my own interest. Those books lead to other genres, other feelings, new frequencies.

It's interesting how interest grow, widening the horizons of our own masterpiece cinema. All within the atmosphere of a creative genius in your actions with what we learn. I call him Guerro Canelo, he's the sponge that doesn't stop growing, a little boy in me. Timid to his surroundings, cautious to assure his safe keeping. An extravagant imagination of storytelling tenderness, produced from undeniably extraordinary moments consumed in affection. Forever unfulfilled for attention, postponing any physical love created a void in him, fixating on fillers for gaps exposed. Envisioning the impossible, a faithful faith delusional to dreams of an unseen reality. As we all do, "He grew up".

It happened quickly, the suffocating demand to sustain society's independent requirements. Suppressing that childhood into notional abandonment. Moving on from neverland came Pops. Colonizing with preparations for fatherhood, that even ahead of his time, no plan would qualify and meet a righteous extent to satisfy the length achievable required to impress all honor, respect, and unconditional love a parent obtains. Love forgiven of all faults, protected from careless agony. An example of a man, solid in his thoughts while sensible on his words and most of all true to his actions. No hesitation responding, providing the stable fundamentals of a leader more than a potential.

Pops always had this concept in deep safe keeping, the idea of a Kingdom untainted by despair that was worth defending it until death. Walls greater than China with an army of history and even yet without access rose a heathen of temptations, influencing the expansion of risk. Another being that would alter the stories told in such ways that sin would sneak in under the shadows into the light for a shine of good time.

Geo, the reckless, deviant torpedo. Lawless in all directions, contained for action and trails of destruction. My favorite Me, the least loved for making the greatest sacrifices under the flickering darkness to find treasures. Digging holes deeper than everlasting loops of space, swelling the understanding to shame. This love is selfless, with judgement on all opprobrious faults, wicked in unforgiving ways, and with no guilt when exchanging souls amongst the cause. The lunatic in so much love with gambling entirely all that is guaranteed for the reward that more than anything includes a peace that can be free of stress. On the quest, he met a supporter who reflected in his drive. Now there was company in crime.

Intuitive with experience because he was exposed to 3 perceptions, inclusive furthering the being of the fourth Me. Comprehensive from his versatility, networking to secure a bigger bag. Gordo, accessible to all the gifts. His genius independently thrives in the beliefs that all love, even that of himself is to be handled fashionably clever. Purposed above himself a greater good, for such responsibility to remain hidden doesn't come easy.

Exposing the safety of our dreams results in a pull from the magic energy he invests. What would we do without a complete version to date? At this point we are all aware that a new birth of myself may arise at any point without an invitation. There are parts of me missing. I have dreams of honest places, memorable times with familiar faces and it's all yet to happen. I don't see this in my future, they're things I know passed but never happened. Sometimes I can take myself back, it requires a ton of consistent focus then one deep breath and I arrive.

Looking around as if lost but I'm not, its disbelief that I bring myself to claim once again what has always been for me. I don't give a fuck if anyone thinks I'm nuts, I know what I know and it's something I can teach. Don't be afraid to spend some time with me, do as I say and just live what you want. Come here, this isn't anything out of this world and by far much saner than the bullshit you got raised believing. Just think about how sure you are of those beliefs and if they give concrete evidence, let's make sure to still respect those before you, for they too didn't know better.

They, too, just followed the rules someone else gave. Learn to be a leader, a creator of your own world, and the ruler of your obligations. Be true to yourself and become a better version of what's around you. I am, "The Great Mindificent." Who are you?

Chapter Three:
GUERITO OJOS De CHICHARO

Climbing back up as the branches and leaves overwhelm my sight, I can't stop chasing those young memories of purity. I keep dreaming of flying off a tree that is barely hanging on the cliff of an oceanside waterfall. I trust that I won't get hurt and that I should be safe. I really don't second guess these thoughts since the water is definitely deep enough.

I'm unbothered by the natural balancing of life. This version of me is young with no concept of consequences or problems. He's still here, faintly creeping into our presence. A face innocent and flawless in the attention of all who orbit on his mindful reef. His mind is like the ocean; it gives in and then pulls. Still learning how to be calm, disciplined, and consistent.

Life is good to him as he floats around freely, unaware of the ways life is praying over him. Deep or shallow, he can coast with confidence from the relentless reassurance of even strangers wishing him blessings. Even those who know nothing about him. Imagine not knowing a thing about this being, but you compliment him as if you know the great purpose that awaits him.

He is captivating, to say the least, so you admire the rarity. A beautiful child, unique and specifically created for God's playground. He watches the world at ease through a pair of green ocean eyes. Hypnotized in rambles attempting to depict a description while he is already strategically building a proper collection in his posture.

Hiding like a secret in plain sight is this playful goofball exposed only by infectious laughter, the only sound ever heard from out his voice at this age. This part of me was quiet and kept his attention on others. He recalls, "Guerrito esto es pa que te hagas hombre." The moments as his grandfather yanked at his copete with identical ocean eyes making contact, staring in suspense with all the love in his tolerance. Made him think of how the transition of the boy he was would break into the man he was going to be, amongst all these average humans.

Never thought of the idea that he could just be a younger version of his ancestors, and there was enough in common with his grandfather to question. Highly charismatic, humble not realizing the effect of the details in his image. Lucious chocolate curls pranced as his grandfather carried him out of a walker four hours into his mother's work shift at the family restaurant. "Sheesh, what kind of kid sits four hours unnoticed, making zero sound?"

Observing a young me trying to get to know myself. Observing an observer who yet knew his reactions revealed all the emotions that someday would force impulse and rage, unlike the calm collection he was. That there would be so much attention to influence his empathy where love grew clueless of the pain destined for his soul.

The Universe began to introduce balance into his awareness, tainting the natural born clarity that came before all contradictions. Life was once held under a concrete slab of security and earnest beliefs. Only he was oblivious to the ancestry of his human history and programing that was being loaded into the mind as time progressed. The family curses supply a deficiency to his person, affecting his perceptive lens.

How to understand the suffering in people's eyes if they masked it by pampering him in compliments and affection. A shelter of bullshit, confused in his own perfection. I could feel his yearn for understanding as if he were comprehending those things weren't really ok, a contempt smile swallowing the disbelief of others untold sentiment. The awareness came from his head but in his heart, there was power beyond regular limits.

The shelter his mom provided with the intention to protect his incorruption would pay the price long sooner than later. She just wanted him to enjoy his stainless existence for as long as possible. To attempt to contain his innocence. As all parents must try to raise "better" than they were raised, unaware that this method of avoiding was a mistake as much as it was opportunity. A mistake to try and control destiny and an opportunity for a new version of existence.

Everything lives at the speed of fate, it's not pain that ruins us, but what we do to avoid that pain. We need to embrace all this; fate is presumed to be out of our control because vocabulary determined this to be a thing of the future. This is a lie; we control what happens next because the future is dependent of our present moments, which formulate all possibilities that we lived in the past. Unless you live your present moment to the fullest, you won't have the slightest satisfaction. You are making standards for the whole world with only expectations for yourself, good luck.

Be a good steward, be for others as you are for you. As your current life is in your own hands and by living it fully righteous, you would please without any factor against your will. This is the way to peaking at your highest potential. Once the flesh can distinguish the force within levels, it seeks the ultimate experience. We are not to look at things as high/low or best/worst, just the force that it is.

Our mind doesn't differentiate until our development reaches "understanding." Well, how to define and be correct when vocabulary isn't only influenced by a specific standard but also by what it means to your personal exposure. What is once the best constantly changes as much as the worst and only pertains to that specific time and no other. This is called history, a thing that passes and can't be changed without lying. So, as a kid, you are conflicted in the expressions you notice but can't recognize, none of this can be as real as you believe it to be.

Purity is where we need to get back to after all the ruination we do to the soul. To understand balance and not fight it, is peace. To find peace makes one complete. Let's imagine the vibrations of the constant pattern as it flows up and down, in or out. Things are smooth until we are confused, unsure, and or conflicted… that's when we glitch in what's unseen. The spirit lives in the unseen and, in its second nature, sends the recognition as a message. The message that there are errors making you flawed, which we call incomplete.

The kid couldn't ignore the curiosity in such a world of illusions and disguises. As an infant, Guero's path was part of the answer to all problems. While one focused on one, he was focused on all. He decided to ruin himself further to understand more by all the silence observing. The curiosity led him to experience, where the more he went through meant deeper limits to construct and ruin with. This opened his mind to often fail and learn the costs. As said, "curiosity kills the cat", and like a cat he knew he lived many lives. I believe it's nine, a Sagittarius traveling extrovert on his eighth life as he is the ninth sign.

The comfort to speak concealed while he perfected his observations. At this young age, it was an abundant world, yet it was a level of questioning that merely acknowledged the adventure itself. These thoughts were enough to maintain him silent with astonishment. Looking at his daze gave people the impression that he was unsuspecting of pragmatic behavior. The scenery changed but the memories sealed in why he would become who and why.

Around two years old and can remember these moments vividly enough to describe a perfect image. During this age, he recalls facing death for the second time in detail, snuck out the backdoor. He stared ahead at the beautiful golf course of the country club, where beyond were the fields he snuck with his father to take watermelons. Totally forgetting a pool glistened where he edged. Slipping in and banging his lip on the border before sinking down, which still to this day retains a scar for recognition. From here, he sank down peacefully as if already content with life and with no need to fight for that life.

He portrayed the freedom of adventure as he looked around and took in this new underwater moment. Blood floating away through the crystal blue pool. This is just another, "No biggie." Mother pregnant with his baby sister she dove into the 9ft pool to save him while dad should have been watching him. The kids silence unnoticed was the correct excuse. "He's fine, it's just a busted lip," said his dad casually, he was always so calm and collected, knowing there were even bigger problems than this.

Yes, it might sound crazy but knowing that life turns at its own will and we can't control it, this wasn't that big of a problem and knowing who and how his father was he blames his sneaky silence and not his dad. He was a Great man himself, paving the very existence of my future self.

This story is better than the first attempted kidnapping at the age of six months old. Yeah, that was just "random" at a swap meet, also no biggie. Amongst us, this miracle boy is the visionary. He physically has been here longer and has seen the most. We don't underestimate his distracting giggles to assume he's immature. To be honest everything is kept collected by him. "I won't risk everything we are capable of with anyone's inexperience, we are efficient above all contradicting measures. This dream is our heart, guarded with all diligence. We live off this." When he speaks, we take him seriously.

Side Note: "Pay close attention if you plan to keep up with the Me's of a multidimensional being. To hear that you are confused in dialogue is a queue that we are clearly too much for you."

The kid is out of pocket. Talks too much, not physically but that alone is already a lot that he's saying. Too elevated for his own good, uses sarcasm increasingly onerous to understand. Everything's a game, chess master improving with precision. Presents a sanity absent from your current conscious where the current focal point of your mind becomes a maze of well-articulated plans to lure you into the library.

Guero loves his story-telling library of stored knowledge for all our conscious senses. In this place where, it's easy to dream big with life hugging you with protection, ensuring every time you gamble through a read under irresponsible imaginative circumstances. Everyone isn't like him to imagine the magic he does.

All memory is intact. Stimulating the sensations in life, a life of ourselves as the ego fed to the cosmos as a sacrifice. Standing for freedom won through ambiguous dreams interosculating living in the moment to presume the future. No regard for obligations to any lifestyle, headless of time and obstacles relying on pure legerity.

"My whole life was influenced by bibles; I outgrew their format and retained their foundation from which I made sense of the stories." So many possible views, obviously could take literally if metaphors weren't a thing. Imagination isn't random; if we can think it, then it's real. Things are not always in our realm, nor are they the current second in time. Know that there are infinite options to accept. A secret unspoken was his connection to the spirits, if alone you could hear the full discussions he has with "himself" as mediating between souls. "This is a place fruitful, given to us to explore and exploit. Much world in much mind".

The shelter supplied wasn't efficient, Dad left early, and Mom worked hard. He had supervision and care, which was always his Tia Chena. As a kid drive-bys were common, not the random ones in the 4's neighborhood but the targeted ones in his direction. Smoke forever attracted his way, which in his mind was a fog for defense. Defense how, if in his direction over family affiliations? Everything in this Universe can be interpreted by opposing implications but his imagination always bright using at his convenience all resources.

Relating smoke to a cover for his ninja ways of fighting harmful enemies. He's good, from the light side, but he does his work in the dark. If not him then who better? How he got there was by curiosity, tempting him to enjoy the mysterious ways of the unknown. Already formed as a wholesome Yin Yang by the time Mom made a change to move away from the 4's. A good kid who saw everything bad, he would outgrow the battle between good and evil to find peace in the journey itself.

Going through things as they came with no way of avoiding what is placed on the path, it's always been the same. There are always obstacles, right now I don't speak, walk, nor eat on my own. All I do is GROW. Letting go is how we grow sooner, right now I have so much going on and new around me it's easy to just take data in, store it for later observations and continue forward. Memories are stacking where I still have much understanding to acquire. Pops says, "Time gives an understanding, and you'll find yourself glitching trying to make sense of past clips you stored thinking you know enough, but there is no such thing as enough because we are constantly storing more, growing more so just live it up".

"Reminiscing POPS"

I believe my father meant that I should go through every passage, for me not to stall in understanding; if not, life would pass with no answer to too many questions. I've learned a lot just living, learning about possibilities myriad to our measures.

Speaking by experience, not a false attempt to learn. Life does what it wants, and we simply react or is it the other way around?

It's all the same thing, and you should learn these lessons; the sooner, the better. The true question has always been will life eat me, or I consume it? I served everything on a plate for myself because "I'm hungry," starving even when I'm well fed. I have the appetite of a giant and I don't know why. I want to understand but nothing is what it seems.

So, what is the point of investing. To soon after just enervate in thoughts of my own gray matter and all that is in between. Besides, I got here first, and I remember what our purity was like in all its original multitude. Remaining still to the eye competently intelligent, it is in the process I hide from an anticipated torment of clueless ideas.

As a fantasist, it was difficult concealing my composure, it is claimed I make puerile excuses held as trivial significance. I did my best to shy away from the spotlight but even hidden that never meant I got to take a break. This was the diversion from derision underestimating the triumph rewarded from above my being. I always knew I was blessed with a gift to help others. All the things I believed eventually came true.

All my memories revolve around hope, an idea of unity. Who would have thought that we would all find a way to get together and be one. I always believed and had faith in what we were here to do. Even when people thought I was crazy, or "full of shit." Overcoming such insults ended up with rewards in all actuality, and that's why hope created such freedom over the shackles that restrained my Final Form.

It is from me that we are duplicating my future, to form a new version of me with less disappointments. I'm the one who is optimistic even after being abandoned like an orphan, wrapped in a battle of loaded tribulations. I'm a lone wolf, that needed to be isolated from popularity. Look closely into my eyes where the long cries travel, howling a plead for mercy. The howls that winds carry across the world, engraving all my intentions in the soil.

All weight is on my back, and there are no replies at the pleading help for rescue. A solitude that lead me to speak alone, knowing I only had myself. The depths of my thoughts have helped me arrange my purpose and goals, which have been written in case existence decides to revive itself. These thoughts came long before my mind was tainted by other beings. A mind vulnerable to a translucent clarity in which its convoluted compass isn't deciphered but rather given.

To live in love with life has always been the goal. To appreciate and enjoy the highs and lows with all the understanding I can condone. To match my morals and beliefs to a style of life adequate to the expectations of a good human.

Loving life became the deepest high for Guerito, walking on air before I was even developed into a muscular necessity. Elevating the common distinguished idea of superiority and unfixed existence, neglecting an uncharted recession where even I, the observer, gets lost each instant between windows of space. Numb to overrated traumas is part of the various costs I'd pay to live over and over. It's all here, the heavens or hells, it's on me how I perceive my feels. I love them both, I'll take them both. Giving all my efforts into living this experience of gambles, I have imagined and created.

It's real! It's real! No one believed me when told them don't speak it when you think it, or we bring it. Right here to one of our many realities, a land scattered to roam all your thoughts. It can be real in a world forged amongst the ideals revealed as the most fraudulent, aiming to kill any being honest to their own truth. Here, we follow our own agenda on sunny strays until night sways away and we do it again and again. Dreams rule the nightmares within, where love conquers the hate that's put out. I teach how to overcome doubts, this adventure is part of who you are believe it or not. Mystic self-form opens in the order of elevation, creating the extensions of sight and beyond.

You haven't met your ME "Guero," the little boy in you? Pops said he forgot his me as soon as he began to wish he was older. I won't even imagine not believing in a creation decided on my command. I refuse to turn over the blessing to a powerful growth where instead, I go to war full force against all pressure, defending my stance. In each fall, I rise upgrading the thrill I seek to condition the perseverance Pops has no need to attend. The Big Dreams they don't "have time for" are mine thanks to the work they did while I "wasted time."

Yes, the promise is made to share amongst all those in disbelief. As my kind self is satisfied to tell the best part of the story. The part that convinces you that anything is possible. Come live where a heart races. To where the highest mountains are traveled and there you find a peaking storm unremitting in the clouds. A peak that will explode in pieces all the struggle wrapped around discern. If what I show was never something at all then what would you call the dreams that came true.

A dream where I provided a victorious success to the legacy of my genetic code. My ancestors rejoicing in the spirit of my soul. Many times, fading out my peripheral desire was the patience for all the work required to extend my existence. I find myself strained by the decision in place to be here and speak to your amusement. Still, like the kid who proudly waits for a gold star just to have a reason to stamp their sky. I am exactly that whole dream, traveling in rotation anywhere, going on and on.

The star never died, embracing a union that lit the deepest crevices, giving fire to the cold and an overcast above the dark skies, illuminating the shadows of nightmares. Closer as it grew to blind the false accusations, all of me was unexpected to reach travels and witness my own creation, as if the impossible thought of me dying to this weak insult was ever accounted for. Laughing in proof, I tell stories to delude my enemies, and scrambling in a dance, suspicion leads to doom concerning your desires. Love comes out of hate to separate its own solitude and stare at its partners universe who it overpowers.

The demons I slay aren't the factors I change, I'll never change. ALL creations of my intuition are never quitting on the progress. It moves so fast; why would I restrain it. Sustaining a movement that you jaded for my failures as I picked up wasted time. Creating Pops was my act to baffle your proposal, sure independence is cool until responsibility sinks in. Pops couldn't see how I told him to grow up if not he would fail. Distracting him with authority and respect, he became a limited version of us, sealing us shut inside the walls of "protection."

Grow up, yet the childish thoughts I hid under when Pops believed nothing harmful could infiltrate. I knew of damage and distortion through an overlooked beautiful land. I saw purity crumble for the greater good of our forever time. There is more to me hidden underneath because I believe in eternity mimicking a life span to gradually exceed further than all the other Me's. I'm still in school learning my lesson, to teach you bullies a focus integrated into the grown you portray as nothings are the somethings you can't dismiss today. I sent out support invitations daily, scheduling my distress as no rescue had existed.

    I don't claim to have done things alone, needing everyone's hesitation was the fuel exploding fears defense. While you worried celebrations covered my air as construction constructed. All your complaints filed are now filled. Giving you Dream City in the Infinity. This all came to life behind the nightmares, entertaining time for the impatient temptation. Watching a struggle give me popcorn instead, I ate a slice of cake. It was easy creating dreams and fighting against waking up, disregard the importance of time and complication becomes irrelevant.

    Delivering a term of synchronicity may no coincidence intrude our actions placing us here with my own words. I saw past the overlapping terrain as countless mountains to hurdle were never dreaded. The beaming of light fixing the gaps between objects covering this journey mesmerized me. To fill all desires, including the inception to an initial realization of emoticons in any digital Universe and transferring into the present dimensions of the impetuous passion we live by. I took it real slow, weaving move by move in my approach.

Chapter Four:
Pops "I Run the Show"

That won't work here. Vigilant towers rise above the scheming games. My fort is on lock, ensure your hopes to think of crossing the boundaries as if you'd go unnoticed. Approval required to obtain permission into the last land of security. Born, raised, and ran to the extent of my best wishes. I rule here and there's no army that can outsmart the strategies that I practice. My moves aren't consistent with ideas you believe can affect the walls I've built. Look up and from below, you see me looking down, you know the climb is impossible and that you are measly ants to a giant. The feelings I inspire are humbling. When I look down, I don't feel greater or more but nonetheless this should be uplifting. To concept, the work I provided just to build this Kingdom on such a natural pillar carved out of a single mountain is unreal.

There's no sympathy for any suggestion against my plan, and there are no changes to digest. I urge one to know that I ultimately run the show, and this will be the only time I announce to air the idea. A good man leads a quiet life, though my presence is loud and clear, making my word final, so don't dare to protest against it. It'll be the first and last time you test my tolerance. I don't instill fear, just sincere respect. Those who obey get their way, as the lengths are endless on the condition of a clean conception.

Anyone can corrupt a vision at the demise of discipline. Very few excel to ever see, feel, or be disciplined. Just imagine what a real thrill it is to lead excitement, carving your veins out as suspense pleads for mercy to stop. A second to regret and fall at temptations rule, this is a weak mind. A majority constituent is in need of guidance, or if that's insufficient, then it needs to be controlled. The easy way or the hard way. I have no problem with either nor do they have a problem with me. We will come to an agreement since I'm a justice man who gladly arranges settlements. No fine print, we can lay it all out on the table but know that I WILL get my way.

I can see you and how you move. My time has passed already, so your plans are foreseen ahead of any structure you plan to build. I've spent an intense time capsuled, studying the least expected reasoning of harm from the most unreal angles prepared for even microscopic fairytales. I admit, it takes a lot to ACTUALLY grow up and earn honorable authority. Everyone wants to correct someone, but only one corrects everyone. No need to even claim a role that is automatic. Intelligence aims at facts and the statistics of a clown winning over; that is such a foolish joke, leaving the claimer speechless with embarrassment. Come correct or don't come at all.

I keep my composure that not even a flinch on my look will you see to continue a game of nothing. There is never a need to engage further than a single explanation; a child's mind does not have the capacity to fully comprehend a chain of events with consequences. Not expecting a short attention span to divulge its wrong sequel, repeating a cycle rehearsed by excuses. It is not age that determines how grown you are but how you carry out your thoughts.

Monitoring any advancements, I'm distantly occupying my spare time as a reflection of our differences. Sweat flooding out my pores, sedated by hard work, that's the true focus. Calm as the same breeze that pulls through the trenches. What you are is what you stand for; time exposes one's purest desires. Emotions are the specialty that I've dominated.

This enlightenment comes towards the end of the track. Carrying off trail, where I thought there were no paths. Here, at this point, nothing made sense, even though I had outlasted my peers by molding and paving my own streets. Assembling a new place still recalling the footwork as if leading was something new and worthy to call greatness. Time doesn't hold relevance in upkeeping to the present moment; all are creations of what I stand for. This alone isn't enough, but it is a start.

The day I decided to be content in my repetition of the things most fitting is how I set myself aside. It's hard not to overconsume substance. Flesh and soul must recognize pleasure and not get lost selfishly to either. There's no darkness I haven't ventured and no light I haven't devoured. A protection to the suffering these pleasures cost is what I supply. Within, one can simulate a new Universe degenerating the human errors of unfit standards. In my own skin, I am acquiring undefined true perfection. A land that quivered in rage found a place to settle silently to my feet. Taking control of the unknown by honoring its true presence. I became energy itself.

I became the source, independent of any conjugated multiplicity. Be your true self, feed what lingers in the depths unattended. Witness yourself never content in the feast of manipulation but instead well fed. Why stay distracted and entertained over creating creation? Don't pay too much mind as you roam, enjoy…. Learn how to be reborn. Experience, appreciate, feast, and move on.

"There's more than the decoy of secrets assumed here for anyone to blame. Weary and unique plots capitalize on emotions, so make the choice not to be the same. Typical humans are gullible and thus ridiculed to shame. Life is a riddle like the only way we take a space rigid and narrow to just last a little in stay. So be calm when elevating, and don't skip on a frame. Watch time in space and enjoy the day, don't let insignificant things limit your joy. Things that sound easy are just that, easy as actions match with the brain. No need to hide so confront all things by their name, but me I circulate here while the wait pauses the day."

C'mon must I sustain a further implication parallel that we can be the same? I've exposed enough to amuse the daycare you run with much need to train. I won't line to par with a being of an impure heart, let alone a sick mind with no sense of direction. I had to make the decision to save myself. Disconnecting from this dimension while still holding onto who I was as I was losing all conscience of the reality life serves.

A battle rages within when what you begin to see is calm and collected. I grew relentlessly in this space, taking eternal beating regularly until I taught myself real survival. Acceptance that everything that gives life is already within, so honestly, we need nothing. The analogy believed that hard work pays off is a fixed idea to convince a mind to keep working for. Unattending the truth of all work isn't always necessary but visionary in what works towards.

Many times, watching the world turn on its own is all the work required. I'd say it's harder sitting still with the thought of, "I'm doing nothing". Not knowing that nothing can be everything! This world is a conundrum… You do nothing and things just land on you lap, you try it all and nothing sticks. Repetition was the key, an answer that made sense, an answer that forgives and acknowledges all you go through, paying no favors.

To be so Godly that you don't even get mad anymore, you just begin to understand the many angles and lessons. By the wait, clarity approached. Resilient thick skin, if you don't have it, you simply grow into it. Noticing that doing nothing is doing something somewhere else, gives a whole new outlook. The world is Yours and Ours. Where do you want to fit? Anyone can build their own, I can let us procrastinate knowing that The Great Composition is rising where no one is looking. A walk through the maze intentionally fleeing security so I would never need a dependency for currency.

Fluently stopped keeping count as if nothing hounded my thoughts. Set for an existence bearable to the notions of living. It required some deeper thinking, check marking every fabrication to revolt. My time passed, but only then did it live. The extent is irrelevant, whereas I'm content with transferring all my findings to a grower. A grower as I'm serving us, my family and the Kingdom.

Lack of unity is where there is no stability, so it's why I unite faithfully, serving the most high. For this reason, I was gifted with power. I'm grateful for the awareness and not losing against irony. No matter what I love, I'll never be too proud to let go. The only way to love is hard, complicated, and manipulated. I can't be that selfish. Motives to leave don't, nor won't inherit; just hold on and learn it so that you may become a master to your biggest failures. Struggle, ponder in frustration as you fight, and take the whole dynamic exploding into pieces as emotions should.

The aftermaths are just as intense, yet different; clean air is purified after the storm. Rewarded to breathe again with a memory marked as a trophy. Creating who you desire to be. Praise your inner best instead of any god; it's he who is within. If you make the sacrifices as I did, you too can be The Great. Appreciate the layout of the conscious grid, and have faith in your divine love as a new prophecy unfolds. I'll show you to be a perfect specimen of human duplicity. Something you can't pocket, with no tag available in worth. Freedom is known as considerably valuable at any cost as the ultimate goal in all realms.

Or you can keep complaining about the same shit. You'll just keep feeling the same shit. Recycling emotions from your memories will keep you stuck when you should pursue progress. Blooming new life, allowing a pristine instant of beguiling. Clinging onto nothing, fearless by your respect volitional for a fresh sense. What you do and what you learn is all yours. Accessible freely by the true facts understood at an instant process. Your own programming is the judge of what cost anything is worth. Willing to the highest peaks for the right outcome.

I understood sacrifice and the effort it takes to construct. To unite by winning the trust of a union. What a great feeling to withstand such a responsibility. Let me tell you how much greater it is to feel such honor in responsibility and fail those expectations. Before this great version of myself, I was a traveler who disregarded any responsibility.

His name is Geo, the me that suffered the most. I sense that there's a close relationship between myself and a version of Geo. I understand his madness but I won't condone it. In his care, two families failed that he tried to form. A share of anything is never whole. With who he is, lays the foundation for who I became. As he tried to form a family, in his errors and demise, I was able to learn how to complete his mission.

Geo tried many times to be something he wasn't. He wanted to be me and had trouble accepting who he was. I realized that it was him who gave birth to me. He never figured out that his time was ending and that it was my turn to be the influence of our vessel. I've kept his thoughts to consult on my actions. I hear him so that I know what not to do. He is my evil thoughts that makes the bad look good. He is more complicated than any of us, this makes him the perfect bait because he is also more interesting. This all makes him the most dangerous. How absurd for him to be the bait that can pull the partner of our dreams and also be the one to be so careless and selfish to just fuck it up.

To him this isn't that serious because he's shown us how simple it is for him to lure, convince, and obtain. His "freedom" isn't free, he had to endure the pain of losing everything else just to be free. His shit was supposed to be like this. Causing pain and confusion from how complicated and complex his ideas are. He can't have an easy life because he didn't have easy thoughts.

I don't want anyone to feel pity for his pain. Just as he endured the lowest lows, he got the highest high. He's experienced the purest forms of love and been so high on it that time stops and nothing else matters. Love is very important at the beginning; forming a fire as big as you can determines how long that fire will last. The interactions of such an impact determine the end of that love. He fulfilled moments when I thought of fulfilling life.

Love is the most beautiful part of life. To experience the stupid love where nothing else matters and you just float in existence unbothered by the nature of reality. The same magnitude was always on the opposite side of the painful end. To be so hurt you give no fucks about responsibilities, and nothing matters again so you float unbothered by the nature of reality.

Can you now understand the empty sorrow of such a way of life? To be ok with just doing this over and over. As if the drugs he had indulged in weren't a good enough high that you must put yourself through such peaks that you may risk everything. You have constant thoughts just to put an end to the madness. Well not Geo, he wanted to get as high as he could regardless of the consequences.

We would remind him of the cycle and the times he cried out for help but we had to let him live his own truth. He's the one I know, one of us completely recycling. No matter how many chances he received he just doesn't learn. Anytime I work with him, I need to observe closely. Unfortunately, can't help to wait for yet another FUCK UP. A loss of time and energy is what he believes to be. He just won't get through the dark. He's drowning. I continue working with him for the reason he's one of us. Complicated, misunderstood but a unique individual living to its own reality.

Luckily, I am a father; forgiving is part of my upbringing. Consulting regardless of any amount of repetition. We must get it right, no such thing as entitled by nature. Ritually spoiled isn't what you need. What one needs is not to be understood but rather to be the one who understands. This will embrace the possibilities for change.

I watched my people suffer knowing a lack of space and time is available at my disposal. Be aware that any mechanism is simply a system within a system. A world of a Universe of worlds. Discussing with the lost me how influence works, and if there is any door at the end of all dead and dark. Is there life in the shadows worth saving? Even he approves the idea after being involved with all that the darkness offers.

I couldn't trust the experiences of his own habitat, why should I be if I was aware of the confused thoughts bottled in that reality. Deep go the forgotten memories of me quitting that journey, a myth is at the end. There would be no Kingdom had I remained seeking the door. Thick, solid gold blending shimmers of the unilluminated fucken fairytales. I will admit to a bit of resentment, although I was completely accomplished in my own journey. This was because too many questions remained present about what free was.

To be sensitive and not problematic, I say he's a mercenary. He says, "Ethically, morals are limitations sugar coating the brutal truth." He's exhausting to understand, but for all that, there are a few qualities that just can't be overlooked. Lost and free is the motto he worships and defends by all means necessary. I admire his fight, such courage in being alone. Surviving as our active support system with nothing but hope, this drive wretchedly moving him all for us. Nothing satisfies him in any position and always updated with complaints. What can you expect when in his mind he's alone with no support, and when he's done searching for answers will be his therefore power he will rule?

I've explained to him before, "Ruling a Kingdom isn't the power to take. Generating fear is incorrect; there is no care for such ideas." It's about what you can give, not what you gave or what you can get. Secure the safety and well-being of all that is yours. Brush the hearts, enticing the soul for its love and devotion. Only this way is the foundation solid to construct up and out. Give yourself to be respected. This is ruling with true honor.

"Ok, enough! You always say the same shit, you sound like a broken record. Records aren't even available anymore; it's now a future beyond ancient methods. Hold onto your nuts and play the cards dealt. Adjust some regulations. Unbothered by anyone else's rules and live by your own." This is the type of response he gives, and he will remind you that compared to him, your story is lame. There's no happily ever after because perfection doesn't exist and to him, this is unreal.

Ok Geo what's a "good story"? Please come with facts and not make beliefs as you say, "That raw shit." It's shit alright, a bunch of horse shit. Just some excuses to keep failing, acting dumb is an easy route. Nothing hard in blaming others, oh no, wait, it's the world conspiring and setting you up. Please Grow up!

Chapter Five:
GEO "High in this"

The moments are always precise to all my hopes and dreams. My whole life, I've always done exactly what I wanted. I've always had the souls at the palm of my hand, and I always fuck it up. I'm not ashamed because it has been enjoyed and lived the same way you enjoy a plate of food and leave it empty. I feast on the luxuries of life and never save a moment for another time. I want to tell you what this is like, and why this is Great.

Embodied the contact as our lips gummed once again, unsure if I was too deep in my sleep to conjure up such longing. Routinely, one touch woke recognition devoted solely as the prompt of a single blundered event. It lingered persistently, knowing its own insignificance that this exact feeling was all I had honestly lived for. Nothing else mattered other than conquering the very things about life that made me weak. The type of things I could easily sell my soul for. It is this very place you should not drift to because here there is no protection just fear, fun, and highs. Remember, if you are hesitant, this isn't for you, I'm not for you. I always said that I'm for me.

What kind of grown up asks and pleads when they can demand? If a story coated in sprinkles you want, then you definitely won't be a fan of this horror film. Blood, sweat, tears, and all that kills. Thrilled out of your own clothes, locked behind closed doors where anything goes. Imagine the dark side to be a field of active land mines. Kamikaze through or just stay behind and watch as you crap your pants. There's no need to get through, you can just stay alone… in the dark with the left behinds. Have fun being tortured tender till you weep, and no one comes. I will look back to see if that motivates you to walk the field, but I will not save you.

My forgotten wasteland life comes out of nowhere. I had this picture of myself watching over my own legacy, putting matters directly in the light for all to see. My throne is like no other, my path of decisions may seem arbitrary because they are and even in all the randomness, I make the most sense. You need to be honored that a real existing disguise even comes from the shadows to teach the world how to function when under a spotlight. I keep this smooth charisma consistent, a replicated motion where my thoughts never panic. Unknown games are my entertainment and pass the time, see me as the residual residue of scum that can't be buried even in the gloom.

Give me a chance to ruin your life, take a little rush for influence. Let's distract all concerns as we create the hole where you'll never come back from. Left to attend sacred nightmares at the place that doesn't vanquish feelings even as a numb sensation sinks in. Yes, you are now destabilized. I live like this. I don't just talk about it, and this isn't some made believe bullshit to scare you. My life is very real; even out of the nightmares, I create dreams. I make the demands and life dances at the rhythm of my choosing, serving my public penance. You must decide: do I give you what you need or do I feed you what you fein.

Here's your store's front line, piling up as pericytes are eating away mindlessly, unaware of the things cooking backstage. I've learned plenty, especially about your biggest fears. Power is on my side, an awareness I utilize for confrontations. Nothing can move me or tear me down. I know amplified pain, a turbulent life without stability. No happy ending dreams for a creature like me after achieving the lowest points. I feel cold, yet I know the only way to cure pain is to accept more. There's a screen between me and everything happening. What occurs around me is as dual as smooth glass that's been dragged through the rocks of a river bottom and left with no shimmer. The words of my life disappear under the lines while time is outstretched.

I'm alone. I'm always alone. Simply a mere illusion of what alive is. A well-executed plot of existence without clarity, certainty, and no fucken sanity. I'm not sure how my state consciousness survives beyond our known abilities to surpass torture. How do I find balance here? In that place, there is a time-bending manipulation of traveling through life and feeling such bliss. I can't be distracted past any infraction, and I know you can't sin past society. It eats at your conscience's grasp, munching on your own intuition, becoming the illusion of your own intuition. Next thing you know, sanity is nothing but a dream, an unwanted relation regulated by gravity, unbothered by the wavelengths of any atmosphere or reality. How amateur to allow one's vibe to determine your own. I chose to refuse your bullshit synchronicity.

God, I love the wicked way of my world. I'm not like the rest, nor do I live by regular customs. I don't follow a basic program, I created that mind field for you to explore. The mind is a mine waiting to blow. Out in the open where shit gets real and not in a sanctuary disguised to keep you "safe." Religion is a foolish answer to an even more foolish question. No need to learn. After all, it's all here, so it's more about experiencing rather than being taught.

I didn't threaten you to follow my rules; I call these basic incentives instead. I'm just a pencil pusher who fires a gun. Too much of anything is bad, I have no rules because there is no risk. I'm taking souls with me for the sacrifice, let's all sit on the edge of the horizon. Get lost in the daze of today and love it like a drug. One, two, three…. JUMP!

What a Great feeling of suspense flying off the cliff. What you don't know is that the feeling in the pit of your stomach will never go away. I know you see a bottom where you will clash, but this route takes you straight through to the underworld. The pain won't end, and the great times will live forever. I'll have you know this isn't the first time I've jumped and end this simple game.

Ignoring the repercussions helps a lot. I'm getting to know the worst possibilities of my capabilities to ensure that when I unite with the light as one, I made no errors and I make no false claims. Without a doubt, I'll know the worst I can be and there won't be anything I can hide. Concealing in disguise, I attempt not to share that I'm the enemy. It's in my nature to be rebellious; what gives anyone the idea of having the authority to control how I move. I do what I want, I don't care if this is self-destructive behavior.

Where my path takes me belongs to all forgotten pasts. I'm writing letters with no replies, and I'm ignored, yet I feel like coming right back. Every now and then, I get bored with the life I live, and I think of the other Me's and what it means to be Great. So, I take a break from my greatness and go try something they would do.

The other day, I even applied for a new job; in the evaluation, there's an inference with my history that clearly reminds the judge that I only create present memories. You can't think of my past, and you can't create anything here if you're attached to old ideas. It's always the mediocre conformist that makes shit fucked up, scared to be discovered for who they really are.

Are you uncomfortable in your own flesh? And if you say yes, I don't believe you. I'll skin you when I call your bluff and a shrill outburst you won't be able to contain. Let's undress the layers on your body you distrustful, cynical human, we definitely aren't the same. You'll attempt to run after the luring, little knowing this truth can't be escaped. I will devour you patiently and you will enjoy this. I can see the way you melt inside with just my look. The temperature gets warmer as you get closer to hell, and your soul gets lighter as I send it to heaven.

You can't recognize my technique. Have you ever felt a presence that can't be seen? No need to stalk, a minute alone retains enough reactions to stir mud in the water. Join me on the "dark path." It's not a myth; there's a real door out of this world. Yes, it's at the very end. No, we won't know how long it takes to reach it. I do know my way there but this place you fear is the playground where I rather roam. My way represents the light in the dark, even flickering, I'm the worthiest. Everyone else is a mere fickle to the glow of my light. Capable through suppression, once lit rooms combine, my shimmer blinds the sight.

It's true that my end overwhelms me with riches, the cost of this path isn't cheap, and emotions die in frustration. Banging your head bloody doesn't solve a thing, as patience is just the first step. Remember that empty ambient space doesn't fill, forever lacking company and support.

Play the game, don't get wrapped up in being in the actual game. Stop keeping score, just keep scoring. Imagine the whole day is the night with no sleep, like when you stayed up running the streets, choosing not to find home. Working precisely with every move, being careful and the only time to chill was when you dragged the smoke in and let the clouds smack. Choking as you feel an endless sensation but it's the closest to feeling you can get. Adrenaline from the gamble isn't a feeling enough; this is how my life is and this is what I decided to do. My being isn't a color from a crayon box, and I don't expect anyone to understand my options or decisions. Just obey as I command.

I'm telling you what to do, people want to be told what to do so badly they'll listen to anyone. It's such a masterpiece to be me, where the brushstrokes are hidden. You can't see me inside or out, blind ass people I don't even pity you. How can you not see that losing all fear takes you the furthest? Why is it that you just sit there and wait as all the time passes with no action? It's fine, continue to ignore me. Don't listen; be still and alone. This just means there's less baggage as I elevate. You should be converting all that solitude into something big enough to force all doubts on their knees. Once in that begging position, you put your foot to their throat, staring from above where you should have always been.

This can become a real addiction. Fuck those sad days, leave them behind and don't focus on small details. Change your perspective to find something, anything, to utilize to your advantage. Find the benefits of all pressure and your failed past all those failed attempts. Convert the negative into positive, remember that manipulation is for the mind of a fool. Make these thoughts part of your coding and stick by it. Never bow nor bend for nothing. Darkness is literally nothing. A no one.

I'm a someone and I grin because they fucked up. The other me's should have annihilated me as they had once planned. They let me live in a dead place "As a prime example of what one shouldn't be." That idea was an opportunity, all so that I could recuperate my thoughts and spark curiosity. I've expanded so much that I'm afraid that I'll rip into pieces, scattering my sense of collection. Influence is all I need, with no need to force. I'm not the type to not gain a lingering mental fuck. It's the best part, feeling the mind as it goes insane. Gotta love a free high. Give me your mind willingly, the other me's don't have to know how we unite. I've isolated you because I'm all you need.

I will teach you how to master the craft to hallow space. With no worries and no cares, you won't even age. Constantly rejuvenating in the fountain of youth. Here, it's ok to sin. Everyone acts excluded from such wants but it's even worse to be one who doesn't get the full satisfaction of living while hiding their true desires. Cowering with discursive behavior makes your own guilt evident. This example of loss is transparent, you're so deep in a labyrinth controlled and removed to true senses. Wants too are needs. Most honestly are set up prefixed fucken failures. Yes, luring as lessons I gladly took to come to my own beliefs.

Failing is infinite, as success is only one way. A failure has no title within infinity but succeeding automatically names you a winner? How definite is this concept? To help all understand, failing isn't praised or said to be good, but it's worth trying. The only real way to learn is through experience, and to me, that is a certain win nonetheless.

Experience is how you learn, and learning styles are how you experience things. One must uncover one's own truest self and avoid the results that may confuse. Confusion is the biggest lie in existence, causing divisions in your own being. Focus on who you are and how to keep that clear. Don't fear being transparent, especially with yourself. The reward will arrive freely and know that the most valuable returns come from trusting yourself as you uncover the unknown. Don't feel low instead refill, insecurity is as fake as a building that won't collapse. There are weak points and imperfections that can't sustain forever. The pressure of the mighty winds may someday, with the right blow, knock down the walls.

Flex and get big, be the giant in your own confidence, aware that size is simply a fabric and structure of existence. Stampede through the barriers attempting to hold you back, prancing victoriously with elegance created in pure nature. I want you to be proud, wild, and free as if nothing matters but this. Be you and don't be afraid, that even in the dark, one can shine.

I'm here confessing that in this space, I became more of myself than in any other chapter. In this dark space, I taught myself to love myself. In this space, I failed so much that I feel immortal. I was beat enough to know how to beat. There's a special power in beating. It's like a fully charged impulse from outer space. The depths are the sunken darkness that most claim to be blind in. If you find your way in here, you can find your way anywhere.

This is out of the mud, here is the place where you suffer and the answer to that is simple. Don't try and live without suffering because it's impossible. Find a place in you for your pain and bury it. It's not a hiding spot, just a storage where it's all contained. Control those emotions, don't forget they're your feelings but not that you belong to those feelings. Look at fear straight to its face and not a response to say that you are afraid.

This is courage, a mighty weapon feared by the cowards that back pedal anytime they feel challenged. Who are you? Ask yourself every time you think of being intimidated in this easy life we live. Are you a coward? We wake up and breathe and we all have obstacles to hurdle, but we, too, can find solutions. Or do you really want to make excuses?

The door we previously talked about is the only exit, and you won't find it if you run away from a situation. Take a deep breath, strap up and smile, knowing a human is built for war. A human can endure more than a machine because we self-fuel. Remember we give life while we live, and life grows even after we pass. Energy is embedded with every action you take and it's working in every plan you started even if it is left behind, it was put into motion and that ball is now rolling. You live in all you touched, you live in the encounters you once had and collided with. There's impact, and that can't be taken away. There's no end to determine a limit.

When you know nothing about something, you have no reason to be afraid because an unknown has no description. With the anticipation of an unknown event with plenty of source to feed, a mind stimulated with this level of thinking gets shaken. This vibration is so powerful, so fast it feels motionless. Good feelings or bad feelings, no part better or worst. All parts hold a place, and all parts are needed in place. They can't do without one another; together, this is a complete creation.

The other Me's didn't even know that they couldn't take me out because I completed them. I have them beat with this understanding, even if my way defines me as "stupid," it's my way that I continue to sell. I'm a bad influence, but showing others my ways improves my own technique and today, I'm more powerful than I was yesterday.

I'm here for the adventure, the danger, and the money. Not some regular money, I want the kind that comes from art. The kind that is collected and preserved for the sake of sport. Winning is not enough. I've won at the highest levels and I wasn't impressed. People talk about legends and tell their little stories. How can something fictional compete with me, I AM THE TRUTH. I am the main character because I made a choice to be so. I wanted a good life, so I gave myself one.

You have two choices: to entertain or to be entertained, so do you want to get paid or be the one who pays? I welcome payments in all forms, I charge with time and interest. Time where you can't see the exit loaded of dedication. Clear your life plan because an inference is impossible to scheme. Purposely, I work patiently, schooling in real peace. Just break from connecting and build your vibration shield, spend the solitude creating your form and who you genuinely are. Having all the time to feel yourself and envision the life you honestly dream on.

I'm him, not ashamed and that's the only way to impress, so I continue denying anyone's idea to fit in. I'm in this bitch and only I can take myself out. To an extent, I'm honestly still lost because I found a way out and decided to stay within. I found out who I am but still haven't understood why I am how I am. How is it that the soul can transcend through such lengths of different dimensions at once, carrying multiple memories as they all mesh as creating roots to a true you?

So many visions wonder in my creations that there's no need to do drugs, my life is the drug and, in these ideas, the only thing I find difficult is to care for others' ideas because they kind of seem inadequate with a lack of imagination. To me, everyone is a mere fickle to the glow of my light. My light represents the true nature of living. I have suffered and even in the darkest places of my thoughts, I persevered.

Falling in love with living leaves no room to share with singular pieces. Closing my eyes takes me away to any place I see. You and I don't carry the same blood, so you'll become infected. Confide without agitation, embosom as no judgement for your imperfections. Invasive is the poison that spreads across each casing. My reflection is embodied in your soul, with written scars on your bones. If you sign death contract, enter through the exit door and be vigilant of the habitat. In imminent danger, I observe the errors that convert one's ways. This opposite will calumniate you without true knowledge. Deeming your confidence while you become a disbeliever.

I am a traveler who wonders the mind. I am the one who takes from you and causes the disbelief. Even within all that doubt, I compelled fate to look at me. Fate is what desires entertainment and with nothing to film, there is no movie. I tended to live my life for every single second allowed. Never holding a thing back and always risking everything in order to film the greatest moments.

In the greatest moments, you'll meet your greatest weakness. These are the things that can keep you from finishing with a victorious legacy. My inheritance was to show women the definition of Greatness. To provide a perfect moment for a complete unattended circumstance. That in her darkest place, I shine the brightest light. To remind her that beauty is a fleeting pleasure. That her moment is now and that even the most stunning can't escape the wrinkles in time.

The price to pay for a time worthwhile is a debt that leaves an empty hole within. It's a memorable pain that will outlast the pleasure of joy in even the love of her life. I am not a lie but simply an ugly truth. Deep inside the depths of each and every one of us lies an illusion of being exceptionally separate from the rest. To make you my one and only would be a waste of such a savior. A mockery of the generosity from which love forms.

Can you blame me for wanting to share? It is in my nature to exhibit the shadows that dance in this ugly world and not care how big or small these shadows become. I feel that it is my duty to let you down so that you may accept reality. We are imperfect, and accepting those imperfections brings true greatness into our lives.

I'm still the same me, decided with a firm post. People want to execute me for apostasy, saying I bring false hope. They fear a population disloyal to their command. Laws, religion, and jobs all puppeting your character. Giving you all the real drugs to stun your growth, your foundation is met by false accusations. This is all vital for who you really are and what you're being kept from becoming. Demassifying truth, a single truth breaking down into splitting ideas. What excuse of a tenebrific beginning.

Formication comes crawling like itching scabs. Perception is the clear remedy, so make it tickle and don't be so serious. Laugh even if you plead insanity, but do it with legerity. Sly by between fingertips and when things are bad, consider them good. You learn most if you fall, no one will hold your hand if there's no support so have a little faith on what you can.

This advice doesn't come from evil, as people believe. I share my ways, teaching how to abuse and how to come up from the torture. Hustle the mind because this way is convincing. This way you'll get what you want, be a getter and when you decide to give you shall receive. Come dragging or don't come at all, give all you have. I want time that's worth more than you'll ever know or understand.

Time is slow, there's no rush when in the dark lessons are learned. Here perfection brews, sometimes the answers don't come right away and for all you know this time isn't about answers at this specific moment. This time may be more so about being the necessary time to simply think, to me it's not knowing what happens next that feels like living. Love life, breathe, take it in. Oxygen inhaled profoundly, enjoy this as if you'll never breathe again. "I said enjoy, so don't even think to suffocate just yet".

Experience what's coming; the harder it gets, the greater the pay. This is a dream worth buying; it left me without anything inside, but I am now able to give everything. Endless help for you all at the mercy of my sacrifices. I fucked up so many times that those benefiting from me feel I owe them. They aren't aware this was planned, plotting at their expense as if I didn't need them. I always knew in my heart that the hard truth would put us all in another dimension, a new bracket. A different life, one worth living where this suffering finally paid back. How ironic that dollars come out of this pain where love has no price. Can I get it back, all that purity I once had?

I lost because of too much hustle, occupying a massive portion of my time. This lane seems selfish and not a single person stops to think how you are driven by the guilt to feed them. They don't believe in love being capable of sacrificing all for another, but I remain in the glory of loyalty and honor. I'm neither a buyer or seller of a false while. I absorb the real you and extend an original translation with longevity.

Don't forget as I consumed you during our darkest times. How everything used to be a mind fuck with no guidance. I was the one who let you catch your breath before sinking us for some drowning. Each time, it was more intense, each moment brand new. Each time, stamina grew as the lungs filled. Obsessed, since for whatever the reasons were, you escaped my grasp. I myself couldn't decide on what the cosmos had already aligned as purpose.

Everything was meant to be and I saw this before I did it. Noticing doesn't necessarily equal existing. If you only see with your eyes, you're easily fooled. This is equivalent to only hearing with your ears. Don't be desperate. You have a heart pumping to the beat of your soul, hear but also listen. This way, you're heard by yourself in the touch of eternal energy. All power is within and without, loud with no sound. I enjoy space to be loud and obnoxious. Home is loud, the sound of my frequency echoing down the halls holds authority. This lets people know I won't allow defeat. I will always remain present, even if non-existent, hiding what is truly invested.

Do you feel fear of investing in you already? Make use of that pressure and take everything it has for you and it's time to disconnect. Don't seek connection, it's a waste of time, so just take your time away to repair your thoughts and create THE CONNECTION. That creation will become the motivation to keep you pushing through. What better motivation than yourself?

Don't you dare let hope misguide you, because I won't let a mercy stray from concurring your soul. es, I am despicable, and at times, I feel disgusted by my own existence. Truly lost in an infested pit of pain. The curse, if there is such a thing, is me.

No need to mention the obvious interactions from what came out of the drug binges that I "Studied." Tormenting my mind is my favorite part of existence. The outcomes never feel worth it because at the end of the day for as good as shit is, life can make you feel shitty any given moment. The bodies I dragged to feel the illusion of greatness, I don't care. It was always savory.

Explaining to anyone is clearly worthless. It's the most ridiculous thing to convince anyone to accept that you are going to destroy everything you touch and that it should be perfectly fine. I can see you not getting invested. The structure I stand for is too far gone to restructure. To me, what other people do, DOES NOT MATTER IN YOUR SELF-DEVELOPMENT. They have their own journey with their own capacity. You have a ceiling, I don't, you can do what most do and climb up a ladder, find your place and get comfortable.

I'm not a conformist; thus, the top will never be out of my reach, on the contrary, the top is under me. So how can you compete with me, keep in mind that I don't even sleep? The only time I close my eyes is when I blink. The only moment I fear more than heartbreak is when you believe. I'm waiting for my dark little place in your small little world.

Here I sit watching death itself run from me. I wonder, if from your perspective it's possible to distinguish my true qualities by the outline of my shadow. I played along but didn't get played by a spotlight over casted in this pain. I made many mistakes and hurt tons of souls, but I consider these the sacrifices that led me with open arms to an aberration of flagitious times, a true redoubtable occult. I know what it feels like to be broken and torn and this still resonates in the pits of an abditory, hidden between life and death, Nor heaven or hell.

Always keeping the irresistible desire for freedom to the extent that the shackles of guilt melted off my bones. It was easy to vanish all grudges I once felt had reasons, these were movements happening within the time lapse, which gave birth to a new me. The real me, born out of agony, succorance and despair. Now, with telegnosis abilities provided by this helix that ferociously tugged and toiled amain. It was precisely following the storm that made the light shine in me and demonstrated true clarity for me.

Here in the storm, I was holding it all together. The particles of my living flesh sticking to each other as if gravity had spun me back into formation. In tune with who I was and who I wasn't. In this darkness, I shined, for I knew the omnipotent prophet destined within. I could not be a prophet of someone else's tales because I speak strictly on experiences. I hunted and made my task to never forget. Memories of atoms chained in my past life's floating within and without. Like an ion charged by a loss, gaining everything by losing everything.

Welcome to the illusions of my sanity. I knew I was in a simulation as the main character. Although I was limited within my own story, it would be told exactly how I wanted. My energy combusting with such force I was always glitching. Maybe the 99.9% atoms is exactly that 99.9% atoms and the remaining .1% was the glitch. The disconnection between me and God. The purest me, my final form.

I told myself to make darkness your life, and your interior will crumble because of the love inside. I'm never going to understand why we would make something bad worst and further yet do it consciously. If a light hovers amongst your essence, you demonstrate the light that illuminates the depths of darkness. I was chosen and spoke to a higher power without religion. I met a God within and learned of the power we must create. I have ideas, thoughts that I'm watching manifest themselves in front of my very own eyes. My words levitated into actions as the plays transformed into realities. This is a feeling I want to keep.

Dreams don't last forever, so those little ideas that spark interest in your heart, go and place action on making them a reality. Want things enough to risk it all and now apply your all. Play the BIG game, be like me and gamble on a match you don't feel you can win. It was never an easy task to detach from the control fear had on me, but it became something GREAT.

Here's a warning: as the heavens open for you, hell does too and believe it's a fair game. The whole world doesn't want the good; therefore, it will constantly bombard you with reminders of being low. Attempting to lead you into depression as if you deserve it. Forgive yourself but work, do better, and be better. You must stay ready so that you never have to get ready. Shine with your hard work and to do this, you don't just show up to work, show up and win. Winning is everything, and to learn to win, you will also experience losses.

I did a lot and learned even more. I had control and because of this, I allowed less from others. My expectations for myself became so high that my lowest efforts were equivalent to an average person's best. I left behind the conformist cowards looking for easy. I couldn't be a person attempting to hide in plain sight, so instead, I became a winner with no recognition. I'm in the shadows and the credit didn't matter. I have no need for trophies when I possess the greatest reward. I have intuition and the means to exceed. I always saw the finish line and it felt good to finally end the race.

That vicious cycle of stress ate me alive, snacking on my old insecurities. Fuck that. I wouldn't live like this and decided to get rid of all of it. We are bigger than expectations with reason that your perception of who I should be is a fraudulent invention. I am myself and this is an illusion in the dimensions of wisdom. If you dare to argue differently, go and experience it for yourself. Discover how to truly consume substance. Find out for yourself and don't listen to what I have to say; create your own story. On this journey try to preserve the true being within because if it's not told in your own words how can you ever honestly defend what you have to say.

Chapter Six:
Who am I "The Opening"

    Until I say it's over, this is only a taste for everyone to snack on. I chose to dip more than a toe in the ocean because I knew it was filled with life deep in the crevices where light doesn't shine. Although I understand depth, the world for me is small, I'm way too fucken big in this space. There are different colors in my soul that taunt this life as I live in a different place. It took many of us to get answers, but what set me aside was that I kept pushing and never looked back. I searched until I found it. I couldn't let doubt eat me alive and because of that, now I walk on water. In scripture, I paint pictures that engrave metaphors. I create opportunity by giving everything a chance.

    I give you answers and if anything is left untold, call on me. I'm everywhere but no longer roaming. I can take myself to any place I once went, retrace the exact motions, and appear in the blink of an eye. I know where I'm going; I am not invisible. You did always look right through me. I hide nothing and for that, it's all crystal clear. I really hope that you understand as my vocabulary shrinks to an overpopulated level since this place is honestly the most difficult realm to practice. For this reason, it's where you can easily get lost. I'm attempting to educate some order, willingly set you free knowing you belong to me. I am YOUR own purest form walking amongst mortals. Inspired to be inspiring and for those who don't hear me, you will learn to listen.

    For now, just keep reading me, watch me in your life. It's possible to find news from exactly nothing. Nothing is valuable to someone, so if you don't relate take yourself there for the sake to concur. Remembering is what reassures any person of anything. Take density and make mass. Power raised in the arts of patience. Learn the behaviors of a gentleman as he takes a flower to a lady. This lady should know her role and receive this flower, NEVER tell a gentleman not to give a flower. To avoid mistakes, I became more selective. I would not fall to the mercy of any disrespect, the day I give a flower, it's because I know I'm in control. When is one most in control?

When no one knows you are in control, you have the most control. I go unseen day to day, moving all the pieces before it's their turn to even move. Momentum builds when you can't stop moving, burning out knowing a recharge can be obtained. The drive must come from a need, not just a want. To fulfill a necessity, create that need. Remember that being still and doing nothing are two different things; now, dying is equivalent to nothing. A torturing blank that I relived countless times in many lives, dying.

It's all more about how I achieved the experience I needed to help the collective population. If you are lost, we have what you need. Come here if you seek answers, if you think you aren't capable of going on, regardless of your excuse. I am here for you, here for us. I am you, all of you at different times in space. There is time for everything because time doesn't stop. Time doesn't wait, right now is the time and life is happening. If you're not ok, it's ok. If you're happy, be happy. During those times you are bored, just do nothing. Everything occurs as it should or shouldn't, and those results create life.

Live your life fully and accept as the clock moves and things change. Adapt to what's surrounding you since together you are one. Doesn't it feel amazing to be whole? What are you waiting for? It's ok to fall. It's more about how one learns, just try again. Sometimes, I felt no one else lived like me. I knew how blessed I was, I cherished the timeless moments. I drowned in life, and it was unreal that anyone would get an opportunity to feel what I feel, see what I see, or even think how I think. Was I truly teaching the lessons I was learning? I acknowledge that it's a gift to understand the power of creation, creating with such perfection and so much intuition at such a magnitude. I AM GREAT, and now I am becoming the GREATEST.

What I was composing is vital for others. I knew I didn't matter to them the way I mattered to myself, and I'm certain they matter to me more than they do to themselves. I held the control, and I am the static up in the air, the thunder down in the ground and the electricity all around. I am energy and it's imperative that we don't go numb, I couldn't let the overwhelming emotions kill my spirit. "You're doing GREAT," I heard these whispers traveling with the wind, reminding me that I am the divine physician. You will witness as faith rebuilds, know that you deserve all of this. My beautiful clusters, I see you and I can feel you. I feed from you as I develop my soul for the realms that I'm supposed to visit. You don't see me nor feel me because all you need to do is hear me. I love you; you are me and I am you. In you is where I reside, with you is where I'll be, and you can neglect me until you are ready, and I'll be waiting.

I hold no grudges; instead, it's understood that a final form is out of the ordinary and may take lifetimes to achieve. This concept isn't a like or dislike but simply different from routine and you will notice the difference between who you were vs who you become. New things take time to get used to, but the good thing is that time is infinite. If you don't see yourself in me there is no need to feel disconnected, there are principles.... A foundation that I created to build the soul being we can form together. A simple mold that I give you the honor to decorate. It's said, "No two people are the same although you can travel on a similar path, it becomes your own." Harvest what's inside to fulfill your destiny.

I intend to convey the parallels of my own living to yours. What I made of life can be done by anyone. I spoke when there was silence and you received clarity. Most believe they need to "find" a God and it's unknown in the direction of insecurities. Under this thinking lies your indecisive conscience stalling from its true nature. What feels right is that first thought you have, I suggest you live by it. Honestly, not knowing anything about the coming gives nothing to fear and like all your other decisions, the results will unfold as they should.

When I used to make mistakes, there was always growth to follow. To better all wrongs, new attempts rose, try different and see what does work. Let's call this calibrating energy. Don't allow bad memories to keep you from creating good new memories. Stay focused and use energy to your advantage to reach your destination. Energy is fuel, plug into the resources which give you life. You have to feel that at the point when these things aren't enough and make this your sign that it is the time for a tune up and REFRESH!

Look for new angles amongst the examples that inspiration leaves you with. I am not what you think but can be a result of your interpretation. What I've done reflects your past, present, and future. Who I become is who you look up to, a finished product, an ultimate you. The aura to feel is basically awareness of your surroundings, heat literally coating flesh to the tips of your hair. Such a distinctive level of understanding must ascend through purity.

Ascending felt Great; at that point, I had worked so hard I wasn't even surprised by myself and what I was transforming into. Everything was rolling up together in transition as the world seemed to fall apart. I became springtime for this and made it all bloom. Feeling everything deep inside before imagining the Greatness itself because I always knew it would come. Now, I was ready for whatever, there was no stutter in my posture, no hesitation in my moves because I had certainty. Everything now had insurance to protect my worth.

I see what comes in and what goes out. The sense I obtained is my backbone and what I rely on. I know me and that can't be taken, nor will it be sold. I obey my thoughts, keeping my temple clean since chemistry requires a stable balance. I feel me and for others with sympathy as I recall the obstacles that tried me. The taste of suffering lingers within success. No soul could be greater than I because I chose to feel when others believed being emotionless made them unreadable. I see right through you and it's disappointing that you would refrain from bursting into tears, releasing that which makes us alive.

No man hath known more love than I. God had truly blessed me. I bared the truth of a beautiful balance in good as much as evil. I was equally dispersed and consumed. Giving and taking, a fight of no letting up, is the only compromise. I went extra hard. I was in overdrive. I tossed on my back all the weight of the endless reps. Excruciating battles just to gain a realization of what to give to the masses. What you want, what you need. Ignorance should offend you, for it is the ultimate bias, a dead end to a two-way street. Unless you go down the roads, you won't know for sure what you will find.

When I went down my route, I experienced with every fiber of my being. The divinity of elevating my living continues to enhance who I was born to be. You can only grow into your own form. My bones were bruised beaten to ashes to become a spiritual warrior who could push and pull a fire, flow in water, mold to stone and fly with the wind. Where you are confident that is your path, this path is the one that will give and fruit. Anytime a path isn't giving you the results you seek, don't waste much time on it; soak what you need quickly and change it. Think of the superior species you were created to be. I know that the Universe is littered with bones as if death is certain but even then, in the darkest shadows, hope will not be defeated.

After these ideas are conquered, what comes naturally and you truly love with a passion will begin to feel like Greatness. I've explained enough to get you going to the place you were already in transit to. This is the contradiction worth believing in. What's in my mind isn't meant to be understood but you should be capable of seeing what's in my heart. I'm grateful to be a feeder of the mind, humbly open to new observations and old beliefs that became what we are here today.

It's an honor to serve an unrivaled mastermind, the creator is the righteous owner of all praise and glory. Through this service lies the path to real wealth of riches. Internalize it in all dimensions and time zones. Believe in what you create, for all I say is invaded by this wholesome presence. Everyone is heard and we all want answers. I felt that pressure as I saw life in a knot promoting failure and false hopes, I confess these failures which kept me in limbo as I was slaving just to barely keep up.

Working for unhappiness as I stacked the space between success and the pit of robotic depression. I was doing this to myself the same way you are distracting yourself by regular people's shit, like a job, bills, "responsibilities," and then sinking further by going out and spending the little money I had, just to get a little bull shit fix. All this distracted me from my own creative self, pulling me away from the certain possibilities of becoming a successful, unmatched being. I couldn't allow this. You shouldn't either.

A life like this isn't conducive to a healthy mind. Yes, we can work with all of this but it doesn't change the fact that it's consuming you. The definition of a black hole, a place where money, people, things, time, and energy disappear without a trace. Some people make the doors while others attempt to talk their way through them. Who are you?

I am a creator and a dreamer. I create the dreams you let slip away from your memories, I decided to keep life alive. I'm the one who never stopped working, and I still have the same syndicate of hard work. All consumed by my mind retaining a rage of energy that isn't even there, yet will always be. I refuse to get beat, let alone be tumbled by a charade of any class.

Here's a clue?

It is the truth; you will see if things aren't going to be worth it. The spirit you pretend evolves unnoticed. Clear to a free direction easily misleads in persuasion. If you do not oppose a natural concession from above, go ahead instead, so don't pretend. This just hits differently.

How I do…

This is how I hit: straight militant. Longing for a battle on any side. Who can you control to respond to your command? When are you most in control? I'll confess the truth of control is when no one knows you are in control. Who becomes their own mold of a form? Now, the main revelation is you when you get through some storm. Leaving a piece of you in each wound, you recruiting is the revolution, a fight amongst yourself because a fight against others is easy.

Oh God how I fell in love with all the doubt, those reactions which held no faith from those who laughed at my face with disbelief. I feasted on your worthless crumbs and made a full meal fit for a King. You dared to disregard my ideas with the intent that you could lure me into quitting. I enjoyed watching you fail, thinking you could keep me weak like a sheep. You must know that this never meant I am a cowardly wolf attempting to feed off what's weaker than I. A mouth given meal I could never accept. I am a giver. You are just a measly taker. I want you to savor the taste of my true nature and why I birth life.

It was an art that of which came before and that which would be after. Here were the answers and at 12:21, a phone mysteriously rings calling on my name. It was time and I was up;

although nothing seemed ready, I was received, embraced, and bowed to for my glorious patience. You actually considered me to sleep in such a long wait. Not I, instead, forever testing my limits, pushing against the grains of time. Surpassing just to set new standards for me to meet. No revenge existed in my soul, and nothing was to be proven from the winnings acquired. The taste I imagined was always more than what I ate off the plate. I was creating an empire in history that couldn't be ignored. In this world of mine, the Me's could coexist in peace.

I fought to be the disciple of the truth because this was the only thing worth fighting for. Exceeding my own physical dimension to sustain a greater purpose. I didn't get chances; I took chances, knowing that no action may come from despair, and I still retained my faith. This living was the kind that put you all in the chest for even thinking of getting into the brain. The shit would never be over, and it has no end. You exhaust possibilities that you must let go. I don't make false promises that I can't keep, and I take the advice to listen to the real me as a whole and never just a piece. I knew the plan for each individual and loved none more than another.

I don't think anyone realized how fucked my brain was. To translate and truthfully create beauty for others to see. I keep my mouth shut and the smooth composure hides my reality. I'm so fucked up that nothing is as simple as it is because I know that there's always some slick shit going on. I face these demons, knowing they aren't more than the I that's given out. I defeat my enemies and call it making peace. The truth has many versions in perceptions; it seems to be a gray area but it's not. I know what I'm up against, leading destiny amongst the trenches. I want you to think and be honest with the truth of your thoughts and how you feel, transfer this in your actions and be sure to be genuine. What I ask of you isn't an easy task, "The truth will give you comfort but in comfort, you won't find the truth." I heard this once and never forgot it.

Put yourself where you want to be. I connected all of me into one by following the symbols of the world as my guidance toward the purity that brought forth the God in me. This me God is only a small piece of the whole universal God. There's a star in every soul just waiting to shine through, and I'm collecting each and everyone to take onto my next life, which will last for just a brief moment. How confusing is it not that one stays in the moment because one is ALWAYS in the moment. I obviate the risk of failures, while you hold onto things like they're prizes.

Be wary that a sad story can come from anywhere even with wealth, people will have their own problems. I was taught by the things I saw in others, and one must be this resourceful to use all our surroundings. Don't even question them and be sure to believe in the purpose they intend. Let observations spark your fire, and intimidation may never put you out.

I have a dream, the kind that reoccurs randomly throughout my lifetime. This dream has retained importance in my understanding of the fact of how vivid it presents itself. In this dream, I face all my demons at once. The light keeps me alive as I crawl to its protection, I bleed out as my breath shortens. The images are bold after each clip, which seems to blink and come back. There's no one there to help me other than myself and either I give up and die or I save my own life.

The dream starts and never ends. It may seem difficult to progress and create an ending but I made it simple and chose to change life's path. I chose eternity. It's a gift to make decisions to do different, to be different, to win a fight because you never gave up. There's a balance within and beyond as the tug of war that must be appreciated. Good vs Evil, and I am aware that both are within, and you can't be without them. It's the reason why recognition of either is acknowledged. Thanks to that struggle, we know variety, we have these differences to teach us what we want. How do you pick and have a taste of your own? A valid opinion that ONLY holds importance to you.

The worst parts of me have victimized themselves to isolate one and not discuss rational decisions. I enjoyed the part where I didn't consult ideas because I answered to nothing but consequences that didn't bother me at all. It's my single choice and made-up mind not to argue, settle, or take you all into consideration. I am certain and there is no vote to find middle ground and rationalize. Understanding is automatic amongst us because we value worth, and with this, we decide on a permanent history. Regrets aren't enough to change what's written.

A wheel isn't made to self-drive, it doesn't run you down when its role is to reach a specific destination. I create the plan for the route, and you will define the location and time to arrive. I made less of a load to pressure you amongst us all. This team was created to resolve and sympathize together to regain faith in what many considered to be a lost cause. After many debates back and forth, we agreed to be individuals, 1 of 1. Perfectly imperfect in all the flaws and before we were even able to comprehend the birth of many, I knew who I was, I was myself and under this scope I transcended.

There is a full understanding of who we are, so I know exactly what we want. My humble self is mirrored as a reflection of the core of who you really arise to be. It's as clear as day when the night falls and both the sun and moon complement one another as they flirt for all the stars to watch. I don't hunt for understanding because the way has been found and nothing is missing. I give you the riches and wealth of my mind because the rest just follows.

I recall once being poor, a vexed memory stunned by the lack of knowledge. Now, you decide to faint at my feet because I'm a wit with power overflowing in erudition. A great mind for greatness since I have no other vision or destination. The rest is forever stuck in evanesce, a blur with little to no importance. I pursued all you see and now you stand stour as the wind drags you away. Before you go, take a close look and don't skip a scene attempting to grasp with such a small brain limited by your blindness.

Be a bit more creative in dreaming of an impossible circumstance. Call me a nabob after you insulted the existence of my faith held by a dream of realities. Such opprobrious conduct for even my biggest rival, all for not having the slightest idea where this all would lead. No one was able to hold me back or keep me down. We decided not to accept a destined life, and instead created our own. Right here, standing solid without a move made in hesitation with no time to think because to create was automatic. Thinking is what a confused being does.

Things aren't conjured like some riddle to trick or confuse, the manner in which I speak is literal and aimed to be direct. Absorb, process and then you digest. Let go and your actions will follow the line on their own. Life is meant to flow steadily, a continuous cycle reverting to your past mistakes where you get another chance to try again. Another life, within the same one or just the feelings of past lives. Believe as you wish but for the sake of sanity, decide to live by that belief you claim. Act like you know what you're doing. When the time arrives for change, do it with confidence and live by the new idea. This is how you hurdle over the obstacles you set yourself up with.

The good in me has no need to get along with the bad in me; this is always a choice I make on my own in the name of peace. Regardless, everyone understands the presence of each other and their purpose. To become successful, they decided to accept each role that is played by each thought and, thus allowing mistakes even if the cleanup became everyone's mess. When it's all blown over, then comes the cleanse that relieves the pressure as to how a soul tunes up.

Some believe that you can't slow time down, let alone fast forward, I know for a fact this is a lie because we all have moments in life where everything slows down. Your surroundings begin to distort as things get blurry and time seems to shut down but, its actually time stretching. The moment seems to take longer and linger, and it's at this very moment that you need to be attentive and press the pause button. Force life to a halt just so you can take a moment to enjoy as your dreams float amongst all this reality. This is the perfect time to refresh with new abilities and give hope to the unfamiliar. This pause doesn't mean that life actually stops; pay attention to the fact that I'm leading you to a command center where you control your life, and it stops controlling you. There's absolutely nothing that you can't do, here you are, the one to set the tone.

I never wanted to be the boss; I see myself as a leader. I don't want anyone to fear me just so that they do what I want, what I want is to feel the force of loyal people who believe in following my lead. We are the kind of people who don't choose to go around but instead make the conscious decision to go through. We would never condone anything not worth the outcome. The growth is all to the extent you're willing to work for. Noted on these papers is who I was, am, and will be. This is a contract of history funded with my own history funded by my own doings. When we decided to come here, it was clear that I had chosen the level of difficulty I was going to play at. Everything has been done with the sole purpose of how capable creation is for everyone. My level is hard.

My history was embedded in my soul, and I made sure to scar deep so things would never be forgotten. To forget the past is something a rookie does not know they are now risking reliving old moments they no longer remember. Each me must perfect an art where they can mimic any level of capacity to make sure others feel good and secure enough to trust me and coexist.

The presentation of my life would never serve as an idea to exhibit my experiences. May my appearance not be a factor in my capabilities and opportunities. We aren't all the same, but we remain equal. However, I chose to chase dreams one struggle at a time. I woke up each day swinging to hit, ready or not but I remained up to try again over and over until the day came and I got my hit. Many witnessed the different stages that I was in, you all saw what I did and the fact of it becoming a done. I want to make clear that if you don't recognize any of this, you are an idiot, but I truly believe everyone is capable of not being the idiot.

Manipulating the world to obey commands made results inevitable. A simple mortal with no ambition to continue living will always create that exact inexistence. It's that complacent thinking which is a recipe for death. Life is filling to me, and for this, you need a good brain, and you really can't blame me for having a marvelous, stupid good brain. I accept that many confuse the idea of being close to being something physical when it's as basic that two sources can be connected regardless of distant separation.

The feeling that you aren't alone, being understood and that you're loved are all found within. Waiting on others, will fail you repeatedly because you're setting rules for others to follow that possibly aren't even part of their understanding. Making things about you as if you are above anyone, thinking it's inconsiderate to respond out of your own. Not that it's a problem but if that is the case, admitting your true nature is the first wise step to take. Only a fool won't admit who they truly are, and I call this a real lost cause.

Conquering myself is the victory I found in life. I'm not focused on your over spilled beliefs. I am that who leads in and out amongst all who I will be, all who I see, and all still remain free. None are contained nor suppressed and that's exactly as I lead. Nothing is forced and in return, all motions get support. There's an excitement for the idea of all to be with me and if refused or neglected, it would indicate I'm not the one.

Magnitude is humbly held in esteem only since I am the consistency of a stable balance. This is what makes a complete ONE. My new life was costing me my old life.

Life is like the seasons, and it must go on to flourish and we savor in its all-true beautiful perfection. Just like the seasons, the different versions of myself are in individual places and each have their own time to create unique moments. They occur once and when attempting to recreate, it just fails and then gets better. Elevating new levels until together uniting as me.

I see me, I think of me, and I'm just that… ME. So, I'll talk to myself, dancing in conversation with the voices in my soul. Don't be confused by the lack of importance since I don't put nothing before me. If Me's are first, know that I do that for you. I know that before I can offer you anything, I need to be good with myself. With all of this, I suggest we try our best without setting a standard nor limit. There's no need for any requirement, so let's be yourself. Understand the things you need because those things are what truly define you.

I always knew that being ok was my deepest concern. Teaching others to be ok is forever a goal. Accepting that shit would never be ok, something is always supposed to be missing, and that all this was coded in us. Therefore, I began to teach myself how not to need anything. I created a code for freedom. These are my own distinguished ideas, those natural ones that make everything simple. I move how I want because if not me, then who?

In my natural state, my eyes remain shut, and my mind is open. The ideas flood with traveling words as the fountain flows constantly with no interruption. This is what I do, and I never expect anyone else to withstand such gibberish. No one else could even deal with the mental situations I put myself in. High level frequencies ignite my state of being, as where in my scenarios, you believe all to be unlikely. You find me to be dishonest because of the lengths capable by the means of any other energy source. We are not the same since the day I understood that everything generates from within, so why would I go and milk elsewhere.

It isn't easy being me; this form takes lifetimes of work. The heavy work makes things simple but never easy. I compacted what was complex into a simple form of intelligence. "Don't break your head by making something simple complex." That's the route to lose your way, and for me floating gently never feels so good anyway. It's just an illusion deteriorating the temple where one stays inside out. A shortcut is just a Band-Aid that will need to be exchanged to continue sustaining the bullshit. Come and learn the proper methods to enhance your life.

I know consistency and how to obtain it. Stability is a wholesome feeling in which one triumphs if achieved. A constant defined by the honest image in how you carry out your instincts. Racing at a steady pace, remaining stable and secure. Be the jogger who paves their own way step by step, day by day. I understood that my work would never end because dreams don't ever sleep. I navigate through life free and always at ease. In this manner, I chased success for the idea of a superior me. Neither here nor there can ever be corrected. The system despises characters like myself because I'm not only the main character of my story, but I become the main character to your story as well.

I force people to kill the ego that keeps them distracted by society.

A system shutdown will rise to deceive a belief meant for me to upkeep. I see past the entertaining screens and choose to flourish elsewhere, hidden amongst the common population walking as they sleep. For me, the mass production cinema of most following a script is transparent. This insight kept me hidden for my studies of the neutral worldwide program designed to serve and obey, this is something I could not condone. I was bred to heal and create and to do so, I intend. Make your own terms and I can play by your rules just to make this whole game interesting.

Getting things done isn't enough, it's about getting the right things done. Initiating with correct ideas, those genuine to the heart and soul, filled with substance and purpose. The mind is a tool that can easily be confused without proper training. The course encircles energy, time, and patience.

Have the desire to excel in reading. Read what you see to know what you have visible on the outside. Read what you feel to know who's living inside. There are no real steps, so I suggest what sounds best. It is what people hear about you that they'll believe. Know that what you actually do follows you like a shadow; it reflects the control you possess, and no one will ever know that but you. Only you know what you do.

What lies do you withhold untold that support a false admiration as a human, one can't be translucent about the frequency of divine energy you carry inside. For one to abide by my might is a simple request not to fight who you are. What you aren't is a waste and far from a stain. However, a smudge marks its presence in every instant location.

All work itself is a reward, a collective dialogue with its own certain elements. This is an instant reminder to set aside a copy made for my personal collection. I found many methods to learn lessons, always feeling failed to get success. It made no sense to do good and be bad, humans make messes, but I am not human in all my perfection. I created situations filled with all that life has to offer.

I kept it hostage in suspense as I let out a subtle laugh that concealed what I plotted. To take over the world was prancing in my brain. The flicks captured throughout my life are like old movie clips, black and white stacked as my memories suggested in ancient times. Then being not here or there but better yet, I am everywhere.

Chapter Seven:
Risky Business "Play It Safe"

You are safe if you don't make a sound. Things got rough, the world as we knew had changed. This is still unknown whether the conspiracy was a test or an outbreak. So many ideas made it difficult to know what was real. Even the things I felt paused in disbelief, nothing made genuine sense. It was like losing your vision; that didn't matter with everything I could feel. I knew what was real and I could see through the storm. I created the storm, and the world knew this. There was a Great battle of good and evil and this was just the start of the war. Had we really barely begun to see? I include myself with you in this table of thoughts, discussing possibilities but at this point, I won't just gamble on these possibilities.

The Universe is more important than a single timeline. Speaking of importance, let's be clear that the only way to get anything is to pay for it and know that it'll cost more than you pay, Gordo taught us this. This kept us cautious of our decisions and actions. The stage I'm at requires certainty. Safety is my priority, and accomplishing it is a given. It's for this reason I am stocked and equipped and always have a plan. I see the way out and make one out when I don't. I've been taught by all the Me's and their talents, if you call it. I've made one that rides solo, the solo only benefits those who belong to him.

There aren't many. It's a tight knit of us who pull the strings. A private group hidden from the rest. Little do you know you attend our events, eat the food we serve, and play by our rules. You stay confused, unsure of who you are and what you do.

Under these conditions, how could you even see us here? How is it that we move? When did we move? Where are we and what time is it? Currently, it's a full moon, the sun is out and the kid in me invents these moments all with an immense imagination.

It's bizarre to act lost, fidgeting back and forth in an act you think I don't see. Is it sarcastic to say, "I could feel and not have the luxury of emotions to be moved by your fidgeting"? It's comical to hide in the shadows outcasted and have a laugh at those in the light, gleaming as you stare. I have a plan and I will take from the poor, and I will take from the rich just to give it away to life. You aren't even allowed beneath us, you are simply away from us. I don't give credit and buying out isn't an option. We manage the populations, manipulating supply or demand. Our belief is that money doesn't make you wiser. Money makes you stronger or weaker depending on what you know. Knowing is important and I want to know what you know.

I know that the percentage of lost civilians is high, you all need someone to help you. Hypothetically speaking, the power to help is ours. So technically, charging as much as I can is more than a reasonable price. Luckily, even we feel the desire to share the harvest of our own work. You get the help you seek by paying a small fine and a fine print. A random subagency will contact you based on all the forms you've filled out. We have noted your deepest concerns and desires without your consent.

More than likely, you will receive a letter in the mail demanding a response; from down the street, I will watch your reaction as I include new notes in your file. Observing all body language but more so what I think of you. I know your common basic ways and the bullshit you claim as needs. A sell out, cheap by the price and just quick to write off your soul.

To feel bad accomplishes nothing, a handout solves less. You are a black hole taking with nothing to give. This is why the moment you come lost, I take advantage, I make use of what you can't. Making nothing into something. It's the concentration that creates a pure moment; not being disturbed is true momentum when attention is paid to the right specific time. The place I stage is all Hollywood, and the curtain opens for all this to be possible because you're uncertain and unentertained.

I didn't just wake up one day and become this beast, killing everything I do. Shutting down the scenes I attend, and you'd think my presence did cause the change suddenly? Many believe it took hard work, but for me it was light weight. This is only my beginning, made with many sources who fell to my ownership. Possessing alternate realities, I am the main character in your story. Jumping into your world, navigating through the fractions as I saw the landscape change. I have exclusive access that most could only dream of; some say, "I'm privileged, gifted with riches I shouldn't have." How do you have the nerve to ignore the fact I worked harder than anyone can?

How can you put a value on the time it took to create such a life? What price would you pay to exchange the current life you live for the one of your dreams? What would it be like in the world you create for others to live in? Are you even capable of not only creating for others but also attending to all their needs? Does the idea of serving others for an eternity in exchange for the life of your dreams still sound appealing?

Possessing alternate realities has a few health risks. Moods swap simultaneously, and it's your job to rein in them. Learn each idea to control how you move. Scattered beliefs disagree on the discussions a single thought could support. Instead, we united to make one on an extent so deep that we have no problem handing the reigns to one single version of us. Combinations come easily, so I'm liable to swap thinking and argue with myself just to have the right answer.

Did I really make it look so effortless that you can assume I don't deserve what I have earned? I now wonder if everyone I encountered on my travels understood or could, at the very least, be aware of what the fuck was going on in these travels and why it was, I who was doing what they wouldn't attempt. I had that feeling of when you outdo yourself, the final breath of relief as I was outlined with my divinity. Am I clear that I am not better than you, but I am bigger. I'm the one to always get people to react, getting the best of them as I take them out for a walk without their ego. I bring you to come out of your element just so I can disrupt your Zen.

Don't question the safety of those around me. The community is safe, for I'm a stranger to their impact on this simple planet. I host a deeper sense, unaware of an existence spared to fill the room. No offense to you but I'm uninspired by a route excusing pity, indolence is up to you. Don't act hurt over being exposed because even if you can affect me in any way, I remain unbothered. In reality, I wasn't even ever really here.

Physically, I showed up and was notice but I gradually vanish as I taunt your amusement. Distracted and consumed with temporary moments, my presence is unattended. There is so much going on around you that you can't treat your emotions, and this is making you unaware of what is at stake.

Turn everything down, you will start to hear the whirling as the wind builds up. The more I give out, the rumbling grows louder and louder, pressing chills up your skin. You'll want to go out into the storm and feel it, but you know not to disturb it. Something is happening and we feel the power that's growing. I feel what I hear. Vibrations are the most untapped source of power, and I came here to wonder. Guilt breaks the bones out of its flesh with no effort in a war of reason vs self-reflection. I create my place to complement the actions as followed:

"An illustration demonstrates with ease, but it's those very moments captivated by the naked eye and not only with the mind."

Together, we push and in me the small unit forms a leader. A solid being trained by evolution who carries hope on its back. Serving the revolution that gets together again in the thoughts. This place to plot does not require a physical scene but what has been seen allows ideas to be born. During these moments, I felt who I was and who I wouldn't be. Just speaking about this makes me look crazy, but to some, I am a genius, which intimidates your intelligence capacity. You will question if you can truly keep up with my move or catch a play before I fade.

Once again, software upgrades occur with each response. The persistence of 9-year-old me is unmatched. Guero made sure to have the ideas needed to continue dreaming. The hope in him never dies because in his reality, the end doesn't exist. He is the beginning of us and still remains within for everything that followed on my end.

Automatically, Pops processes revising, which is an instant reaction because he has the map laid out of all the land. Injecting your veins with limited capabilities, deciding for you how to stay busy and when you're allowed to rest. Exhausted, you'll have little to no effort to oppose decisions and let alone investigate for explanations. I am a true virus. A Great father to the Kingdom.

At this point, invading you may feel like the drag that this is, you'll become entirely drained and it's all right on schedule. You couldn't have prepared for the art of my war. Me, with one final flick, would clearly be abusive and unchallenged, in your simple language, I'm just a bully. What would be unfair would be to allow anyone to stand in the way of my success. I will only fight against myself by protecting my integrity from my own wrong decisions. The heart and soul belong to my angel, and my mind is still where my demons lurk.

Geo kept those demons in their place and decided when they could play. I know you have opinions and a biased outlook with the equivalent understanding of a nobody. I just don't care about what you think because I know how to give meaning to a life worth living and still see your side. The fact that I think of your possible reasons to coincide with my own is why I'm who restores balance. This is my call for you to remain fragile. I am a menace but a fair one.

Life is nothing without freedom, and I'm also the one who controls it. I choose when to take away your freedom but the real plot twist to that concept is that my methods provide true liberty.

They teach you how to have a voice that's subtle but perspicuous. To think you know a little more would be naïve, so I showed you how to let your light shine.

Imagine my character unpeeling like layers of an onion. When I first discovered my whole self, I kept my identity a secret for an exceptionally long time. I took the time to be completely alone, marinating in appreciation for my understanding. There were forgotten ruins in this world in need of my touch, and it was best that I did this alone and unescorted.

Being secretive is my coat of invisibility that gives me leverage to the extent that I can give you a head start and then go catch up. Don't create an idea to rival a creator. So, when I say fall in line, know I will give you the proper response. As much energy is gathered in me, this is not a fight you can think to have, and this is sooooo unfair. The collective source of energy is my power to wield as a weapon and a strategy to defend. I understand logistics and the capacity of the creative being I have become. Any ideas you entertain to work against my methods really carry no threat because when it's all said and done, what I come out to do works.

I don't feed an ego like an insecure teenager awaiting his credit as he flaunts visibly for others to see. Think of the true power of a person who gets shit done and although not credited, he continues to give. I am unconditional and anonymous in my giving, donating because it's the right thing to do and not because I need the world to acknowledge I'm good at giving. There's a shift in consciousness when you hide from a spotlight. Have ingenuity because life isn't this big conspiracy, instead it's a mirrored belief of pure sense. Everything begins, entertains, and just halts to an end.

With Guero in me, I have no end. I run and won't stop running everything that I am. This thinking created a fight in my mind against humans very nature, which caused glitches to exist in my programming. I knew it was because I was forcing a great power to comply with me. A power beyond this mortal plain. A full-blown war inside of my head.

For each fight I had with myself, I was risking not coming back. Knowing the subject of my beliefs was all to entertain me. As the time accumulated in my own dome, I accessed more information. Dancing with my own demons and showing them no fear just to enslave them to my cause. The power grew, and my excellency may be formed from my bidding and words. I competed with greatness by vowing to protect the people and provide for them. This is how power was acquired.

I had realizations of life and purpose subjected to a substance. An addiction to time defined by my own schedule would always be the only time spent. Value is what I buy, and I have an understanding of my qualities. It doesn't matter how much because it doesn't mean it'll sustain its worth. My theory is not about what I want. It's about what is right. I don't think of repercussions, instead I enjoy what comes to be of my decisions. Regardless, I can't predict the future because it's yet to happen, but what I know is what I'm going to make happen, which is CREATION.

Creating in the present molds the future. For this reason, I always did the best to my knowledge, and I believe that you, too, are doing this exact thing. "The best that one can with what they got," and what we have is energy to exchange. I have a fear of being complacent, refusing the fardel of a systematic like where you're told what to do, how and when. Think of what is more relatable, what you hear someone else perform or what you yourself conduct and tune in your own memories?

It's always your own work that allows you to build morale. Having multiple opportunities to become a source of your own tunes. Wants and needs are led by what is buried in your soul, and that is your truth. I suggest you put an end to the psychological warfare, stop debating what you should do vs what you want to do. Don't be instructed by the things provided at your feet and assume this to navigate the line you follow. Strive to learn how to control your emotions so that you know how to treat the world that is trying to deceive you with persuasion. Fuck being controlled, I DO THE CONTROLLING!

Things may sound a bit dark, but that's because they are. I do most of my work in places like this, in the dark, where praying doesn't save you. God knows I keep full control of these realms for us. All the Me's shine light through the wicked thoughts and depressing corners. The shadows who cast evil scramble in desperation away from my reach in attempts to escape. These shadows met me and knew that lost I wouldn't be. Being that afraid of anything is a cowardly move, as if I was just a piece of a man when I know that I'm a whole.

I recall old memories of me being hesitant, not wanting to change who I thought I was supposed to be. I couldn't help it if I fought against destiny, and it just beat me back. I evolved to realize this was never a mistake and that all change has a purpose.

Of course, it was possible to revert to my old self but there was no fun in that. Besides, to reach my Zen, I need all of this and at my Zen, no one can even imagine fucking with me. I can utilize each proper phase of my past at precisely the adequate moments. This is how power taught me to work, doing my best to hunt on this scarce land. Scrapping up the essentials needed to advance beyond the required expectations. When you ask about me, I am the best.

I wake up grateful, I look above to the heavens with both my feet buried in the soil. Admiring my blessings, I see why I'm here. What you must know is that out of all the "phases," the current me is my favorite. We thought this was all too crazy to obtain, an unreachable dream. What no one expected has now arrived at the place where it's needed. Separate, distinct from the masses and be capable of telling you the truth. This isn't my first time here. This is why I live life with the same certainty that this isn't my last time here.

Each life gets easier, but my dreams remain ahead in this race. I continue reaching on days attempting to force defeat over me. Dragged through the mud, day by day, stressing about who I am vs who I want to be. It's not a want when it's destiny. There's a bridge between the time that is extremely fragile and each move one makes. The loads eventually began to inclusively align with my alliance. I am undetected by artificial intelligence and unheard of by a physical eye. Attempt to understand a mind similar to your group's totality.

Yes, I'm many in one vessel spreading a message. "I know in you many changes rooted from the heart. Leading to places near and far but both with no end, just a start." My eyes are of infinite supervision where words don't explain the wonders of the universe. A system where you shouldn't mold to a mind calling an escape, especially when it's all at stake. The Greatest Gamble against I, The Great Mindeficent! Lead by reason and self-reflection. You can't jam a jammer.

Listen here, this "living condition" is painted to be a miraculous hallucination. I'm just a patient observer jumping dimensions; ancestors rest in my soul, speaking untamed tongues. Ashamed, why must you be a fraud for a lost conclusion created based on the ideas you guessed with no facts? You don't know me, but my health still relies on whether I remain free. There are no soldiers but I'm here to take over.

Free power comes drawn in the blood, lying ahead like a plotted profession. It's tedious to extend my helping experience so others may elevate and make my game more interesting. Coaching you to apply from what's free of will in the hope that this results as a raise of your state. I feel great yet still humble to be a good servant to the peasants. It is an honor to be here with all of them, each and every day walking amongst the lost. Waiting for them to rally and also be Great.

In place is the balance that you, yourself, create and manifest. Set a standard and do what is required to meet at the line, and trust that obstacles will fail to hurdle over a composed mind with a plan. Don't forget that we don't conjure anything; we manipulate what already exists around us.

If I can't show you that I'm infinite, at the very least, I will appear so, not in an instant but gradually advancing. Becoming greater in each precise move, filling the shoes of a Great in my world and showing up to be the Greatest in your world. The knowledge of weakness is what made me strong. Accepting the dance with my demons was to remind them that fear was not for them and that they would remain enslaved to the cause. A wave was not to tumble, nothing existed that tasted better than peace. If my demons couldn't persuade me, a measly human would have to forgive my negligence.

Understanding that everything holds spiritual value, the places could change but the spiritual realm within that space remains. I want to make clear that I'm not against any religion or God. I found God in all things uniting, a tremendous power emerged from this belief as this is how I found divine vastness. At this understanding, it's only right to abide by a genuine sense, an instinctive way of life. Lethal reactions, if encountered by any threat to the movement, I support. This is what I feel like ascending, where in my presence, the proper greeting is to quiver.

I am they, the one parallel to all at once. In little words, embellishing the edges of who I am, which have always been as perfect as you witness today. Things always presumed to reflect what hard work and an unattended mind could create. Not building my vision turned into the public's enemy. My word was success and by any means, I'd drag my sanity to make what I please real. I have a true handle on what I stand for and always see the urgency within the populations. You were all in desperate need of the growth I provide, I'm just like the food that you hear and the thoughts that you eat.

These ideas I condone often bring to my concern if I even have a breaking point. What are the most efficient forms to break a person like myself down? A type you know isn't attached to any other thought aside from what their eye is on. That is the question; it's curious to think of words that will never be spoken when, in my mind, the phrases you would need to understand float. One never knows what I see when I stare into my mind. Everything I did and do is to answer the phone that rang while you ignored it. You reject the annoying tone, ignoring the urgent matters you don't bother to attend to. Don't be baffled to see your desires fulfilled in the life of someone ready to answer the call, paying in full. Life had to play out a certain way, and I was prepared to make the highest bid.

I let many people down on this journey. I used everything and everyone with no excuse for my actions. The functions of my intricate process, with an over indulged personality still evolving the adequate methods to communicate. Not sure if you consider my sympathy when I value your lead. The lengths, cost, and dividends contrast results so insulting to even speak on. I've mastered the ability to turn off any sense at any time yet still be as sharp everywhere else without it, this technique can't be beat.

Many things up in the air, for certain times, have their own moment. I've assured an answer with your vote in my pocket. To use something as elegantly as a tailored suit among a closet of exact replicas is a victory. Commanding the respect of my peers would mean the world to me—the world which already belongs to me and bends to my will. Day by day, I win it over again, making it mine to give. I am a creator who has mastered his craft with the patience necessary for self-perfection, graceful in movement and convincing in words.

There is nothing more to desire beyond what I offer. The most generous gifts, those that are mandatory to me, are owed from birth. I give you my tone to tune, a melody synced to our memories. Uniting the universe is a task I perform in my sleep, and when I wake, I whisper to the sun to rise. The time will come for it to set because I arrive to work so my sun may rest. The moon is the leftover mist of my energy from all the ground I covered during the day, meant to illuminate the minds of those who wander at night. Unaware I touch and heal. I feel… feel…. I still feel.

Together, we come back as if from the little left purity of a Northern Forest. Layered lava covers the grounds where the pines reach heights measured by Giants. My roots blossom heavenly from the vortex found running around these branches. Buried soil is my pain, dug deep to replenish the world if I'm ever lost. Today, I have direction. Intentions on my hands, a natural selection generates my emotions for which I act on.

Unlike many times before me, in your place connects emotions to relationships. Nouns shouldn't direct how one feels, these feelings are of yourself and belong to blame nobody else. It was here where I begun to feel solely on my beliefs and being true to who I am. I feel strong over the discussion of beliefs, this is a passionate conversation to have. What feels honest in the soul is what I allow to be my cord, an anchor to this life. Respecting yours, I don't see a difference to disagree, I can't neglect to want an understanding of how you process.

As pops would say to come and share to "A Free Land," just a humble sanctuary far away in a dream. A place above average, unreached without a walk-through fire where the coals glow at the sound of the beat. Out of these ashes, rewards are born; it's up to you where you lead your path and what results you get.

Forget what is undone from times before. Meditate to uplift the pressure from the soul to be unattached of such burdens. Let the memories drift to wander in the cycle of the air, floating by the cast of a surface unmeasured by the eye.

I suggest all this because I care that there's no infinity without us. For you to see how things connect, you must appreciate a good story when you're sitting and being read to. I see a future and must reach it, knowing the beatings that this will teach. My homework is always difficult, but labor is a given talent and time is all I have. My own two hands get filthy when there's need, although I do prefer to solve with verbal communication; it's the mind that outwits a tongue. I have the pride of a gentleman reflected in my posture when I speak. There's eye contact and I will not slouch or fidget. My character is always measured, and composure will be held. Believe it's a serious case to encounter an individual with such a definition.

I don't want to overlook my influence on how things navigate. Results depend on a world filled with cluttered dreams that overshadow reality. The doctors can't fix me, so all I do is entertain. I'm mind blown during interviews when I meet someone new, wondering if I can continue to evolve. We are all different, but it's my control that impresses you—a genius— while you compare me to a sickness, disbelieving that it's always I who does the fixing. A prescription for a wholesome life is acceptance, not a pill or drink to wash down your sorrows.

The path to reaching one's dreams is easy. A thin line to walk aside some gaps between flesh and spirit if you seek it. Prepare to face a force of nature so beautiful that I couldn't even fear it. Captivated in my stutter is the assurance insured. Secured that the gamble is guaranteed, I put trust in natural selection. If the work was done, persistent and consistent for sure, it had to give back. Nothing to force misdirection on a path paved by your own physical self.

I extend myself on the planet, encouraging order. A population of people lost is in need of direction to teach reform. Follow yourself, not in circles but in the direction that moves naturally to your being. When circles you run, let them be the repetition of looping moments worth doing more than once. May you feel inspired to take your own charge.

You'll feel your time arrive, as for me, there was no need to be pushed because alone, I dove into the waters. Drowning was always a possibility, so I just learned how to swim. Anything else was also treated the same, headfirst. My mind open and ready to consume. Everything discussed is true on the facts of a witness held to a position of sight. Experienced firsthand the endeavoring to help me with my own lost parts. This perfection is whole when accompanied by its flaws like a tint to stain my library of personal recollections.

All the characters molded in our roots create a concrete foundation that must be honored. Deep down inside, we are alike with no difference, but how we lead if you take our guide, may reach the same destination through a different path. The point has always been to fulfill your highest potential. I have no shame and never hide, make me accountable when you feel at fault. It's nothing new for me to take the blame.

Assume I also take the credit for adopting all the blame. Fair reward after showing my face; in me exists no coward, so I own my day. I wake up and faintly bow to show respect. Humbly, I ask for methods pertaining to pleasing the sacred space most take for granted. This is all followed by forgiveness for myself from the disappointments I may conceive. At all times, I refrain from error and remain conscious of my choices. Let's look ahead, create a plan to reach all goals, and then make more goals to keep you pushing. Defend what you believe, and in that work, a throne is built. This is your world where I just live in it. You decide if you give up on future moves or sit back. Buckle up, and enjoy the fucken ride!

Chapter Eight:
Gordo the Giant
"for me, everything is easy"

I was glitching, trying to override everything that I was programmed to react to. The system didn't like the part of me becoming bigger than all of this. Knowledge had poisoned my beliefs and now I had no limits. I took the restrains off that kept me distracted with the masses when all that truly mattered was me. The selfish course that I was on is creating greatness and the world wasn't prepared. A world who I gave no option to and at the snap of my fingers, learned to submit. Everyone watched me work tirelessly, thinking I'd collapse, unaware that inside of me lived a fat, rich old man who needed to be fed.

Gordo lived off the sponsors who cashed out for his ideas, making him look better than he could on his own. "A mystery man who surrendered his emotions who never gave a fuck to communicate effectively or empathize with others," this is how he was described on the front cover of a news article in California. He spent his money concealing his locations so that no one could ever stop him. How could he be stopped if he is on multiple timelines, living many lives just because he can afford it?

The truth is that you can't stop him. Stopping isn't even his decision to make, his energy is meant to live on. If he left, all that he accomplished remains, he is forever rich. He taught us that true wealth comes from the contentment of the heart and not from the materials you chase. Gordo always persisted in teaching us to be rich with what is already yours. "Be happy with those things that no one can take from you." His advice was uncommon, short, and expensive.

There were always huge gaps of time in between, but it was a rare moment when he made an appearance. His influence strong with minimal words. It was like when he spoke, people couldn't help but tune in. I attended a special event in the winter of the year 2040 where he was said to have been paid nearly $4 million to speak and all the man said was, "Your desires are the entrances and exits of your will." The room went silent as everyone soaked the words with hopes to cause a change in their life in his direction. An elder man believed to be an underworld King was the first to vigorously clap praising Gordo when the rest followed. I could see how people looked up to him as he looked down. I noticed that he scanned the room calmly without movement, but his attention was solely on that King, and this was extremely important.

The rest of the time consisted of formal handshakes and nods from Gordo, not another word was said and within a blink, he was no longer in the room. I roamed the mansion, looking for him, confused at his 8-minute presence, but no trail was left behind. When I returned to the main room, I noticed the King took a seat and gradually began becoming absent within the event. The king was stuck staring at his watch and 8 minutes later, he got up without a sound and headed for the basement exit. I couldn't help myself and I followed, something inside of me told me that the energy exchanges this man had with Gordo wouldn't go unattended.

My blood rushing even if I was just risking my meaningless life. I could feel the intensity of a modification at my doorstep, and I couldn't ignore my decisions and bail now. These were high-valued men with more power than this planet could entertain, and I wanted front seats to this show. I kept my distance, but my breathing couldn't keep up. I was only a stairway apart when I lost sight. I panicked as my opportunity slipped my fingers and rushed down the stairs. Of course, to my surprise, they were both there at the end, waiting for me. Nothing was said but I knew the look meant for me to hand over my phone and get in the trunk.

The drive was short and felt even shorter, I feared the sound of the trunk opening and when it did, the King was there alone, looking over me. It was so strange, we locked eyes and at that very moment, all the pressure was lifted, revealing that I was safe.

-"You risked your life, and for what?" asked the driver.

-I replied, "What is enough seems much, what is much feels infinite."

"Infinite I became"

A matte black speed boat awaited our arrival, inside was Gordo himself. This time, the silence I expected was replaced with a "Welcome, your life is forgotten, and I will gift to you the teachings of our ancestors and eternal life". I understood that I couldn't go back, and I didn't care to go back. From this point forward, nothing would be the same. Gordo was becoming part of me and I, a part of him.

For him, the adjustment was instant; with no struggle, he had the ability to absorb like a blackhole. It was different for me to adjust because I was lost in the labyrinths of his mind. Have you ever had a giant whisper to you? Reminded me of the rumbles that a natural disaster conjures upon destroying. The suspense made the sounds deep and long with no end, I'd lose my breath each time, holding in agog. I could feel myself losing to Gordo, but I wasn't even fighting. My last memory of who I was, is the moment I decided to follow Gordo, knowing and accepting this was my end. That day, I died and became reborn.

Before boarding the speed boat, I watched Gordo stare off as everyone waited for a command. The silence broke, and Gordo said, "You don't know me, but don't try to get to know me. I'm far too complex in my depths of understanding, I'm like the ocean, so vast that there will always be hollow space for you to get lost." Take a seat here in the sand, stare off into the horizon and think about how you don't see the end, your perception gets lost on the surface of the fog. What you see evaporating on the ocean surface are my vessels equipped with all my tears, you couldn't fathom the amount of violence I went through to become this soft. My voice is soothing and carries itself exactly where it needs to go at the very moment it needs to arrive. I am what it would look like if everyone was united and working together in harmony.

Success is to accomplish an aim or purpose. I've taken on the most frustrating task so no one else would have to. I aim to get everyone on the same page, but this doesn't mean that you must think the same way or do the same thing. I don't expect anyone to understand, I'm here to listen and be the one who understands. I'm emotionless about all of you because I'm conscious that we don't have the same capacity. There's a gap between human interaction vs how you interact with me. Humans get lost in the experience because they only see themselves as a physical object. I show you how it's not about the object itself. It's about what an object symbolizes on a deeper level.

We are a quality of our thoughts, this includes the things you desire and chase. I've heard people whisper about me, that I say things as if they were easy just because I already "MADE IT." Every time I hear this, I remind myself to be the one who understands and that you empower my growth. I can feel the energy and I've let God teach me how to transfer it into light. It isn't that I'm arrogant, it's the fact that I am RICH. Don't think of dollars because there's wealth in life itself; so much of everything has been given to me that it's difficult for me to be content with anything or anyone. Yet God chose me and made me rich.

I remember when I was working minimum wage, dreaming of this life, and my peers made fun of me by calling me, "El de Los Milliones". I was never upset over this, I thank all of you who doubted me, so it made me work harder. It wasn't just my hard work that got me here, I would mindfully speak on ideas that I knew you thought were too far fetched just to make sure you kept my "craziness" in your thoughts. I created the dreams in our sleep, but I always remembered them each time I woke up. You thought that someday I would "wake up" and be done with all of this, that I would just quit on my life's work.

I was broke and I loved myself. I would break and consult with myself. I created The Union out of exhaustion from splitting us into the whole world. It was as if each time I left a little piece of me attached and I've traveled so much that my roots are connected infinitely and bound to what we are, energy. My air is still... as it lingers around all the minds that have connected to me at each encounter we experienced. Obscure ideas have always existed, which I didn't believe in, but I always knew keeping the peace was much more important than proving my point.

By hammer and chisel, I constructed the empire for you to witness and follow. It was the chunks of stone that came off of me that flew down to make your mountains. You must know and come to understand the depth beyond what you physically see so that one day you can look at a mountain and know that its actually just a symbol to represent the firm grounding from which we are born.

Let's make it a thing to utilize our memory for moments worth keeping, don't be ignorant trying to erase harsh times because those also hold value. Learn to grow and know that if you forget history, you are doomed to repeat it. I know of all the fairytales forced and coded in you to believe in, but let's be realest and aware of what is true and honest to what we are. Don't let the ideas instilled in you with no true substance misguide you into a false hope that can lead you to depression. This is definitely a life worth living, I want you to feel what I feel.

Gordo introduced to me a world that can't even be discussed in your conspiracy theories. You're doing too much, and I'm now one above that's laughing at your distracted mind trying to find blame for your failures and lack to overcome obstacles. I listen to you in the crowds complaining and I sit waiting to see when you'll realize that you've solved nothing and gave those around you the impression that you're a cry baby not worth taking seriously. Get in line and leave your message in the complaints box, make sure the door doesn't hit you on the way out. You are a number in a vast universe, and I understand that.

Even now that I'm here sharing my experience, this will fly right over your head, and because I will not waste our time, I wrote about it instead. You've spent time wasting any creative thinking to prove what the world does that leads to the results you are living, when the hard truth is that who gives a fuck when at the end of the day, you can't control that. The power you have is within and how you put that out is up to you, how you decide to distribute is the purpose of your power. All God does is designate your position, but never forget that it's our job to work and retain the position. Love what you do so that you may be passionate and care for what you accomplish in your doing.

Strive and be the leader of your world by always making yourself available for your people and the extras in need. Realize that true worship comes in sacrifice with your own pain and that answers only come when you honestly believe in the natural will of what is meant to be yours. I bowed down and prayed for this, and trusted that in the silence, the work was being done. The battles we fight must be in our good state and the bad state to recover the teachings we need to progress. Don't let trauma drain your energy, accept, and grow by wanting more.

I am proof that even in a crazy world, a crazy nobody can become a crazy somebody. Almighty God made me a God, and even in this capacity, I am but a grain of energy compared to the power embedded in the purest form that I retain within. The parts that have yet to be unlocked and the power possible are infinite, so I will always remain humbled knowing there is more to be done. I gave my deepest power and those were my thoughts, where everything was put out and nothing was held back. I have no secrets. I've given you all of me. It's my sacrifice to you, to expose the errors flesh makes with no lies. I've given true love in my experiences to never make seem what I am not.

The day I came forth to be true and make an honest being of myself, the planet rumbled. Winds of 200 MPH stormed the gaps of our planet in honor of this big day. I could feel my flesh pull from my soul but I wasn't sure if I was ready for all this. God had his plan and my life wasn't my own to begin with, so again, I bowed then I let go.

Are you ready to disconnect? I was waiting for someone to join me in my solitude because I had outgrown everything and everyone. In the meantime, my bond with the spirit realm was growing stronger, as if becoming one. Was Gordo, when he entered my life, all spirit and no flesh? Could it be that this whole vision was me imagining my future self?

I realized that it wasn't the objects I obtained, the luxuries I had basked in, or the recognition I received. It was the memories, the stories of all the moments that I made sure to attend and share with you. So that every time you hesitated, my life was worth it. Now that I've taken the time to sit and write about all my endeavors, I'm realizing that the dragon I was chasing was always chasing me, trying to keep up, leaving a trail of my touch in the many lives that experienced me.

US, I had enough to scramble the mind of an average being who couldn't have the capacity to withstand such a brutal span of remembrance. A collection of souvenirs is all I have to show for the places where my money wasn't good enough. Imagine a place where I couldn't pay to cut a line and where prices weren't firm. My greedy needs couldn't charge dollars in exchange for memories. For these, I paid with my stability. I allowed myself to float away without knowing if I could make it back.

I recall having some of the greatest loves to support a journey they couldn't even follow me to. This journey was my own to fill. Space, not the fairytale one with planets, stars, and lights. This space was empty, dark, and clear of distractions. Torturing myself with my thoughts as they ran wild, I saw all the hints and all the hidden messages. I knew y'all were lurking, trying me, thinking you could outsmart me. Luring me with bribes of the things you "thought" called me. They don't. I stopped giving a fuck a very long time ago when I was forced to end my bonds with no opportunities to fix my wrongs. There was no way I could travel with all the guilt trapped, so I just let it go.

I could never let myself go. This experience was making me realize my own traumas of all the shit I've put aside for such a long time, I never gave myself the opportunity to heal. At some point, it was okay to ignore it as if it had never happened. Then I questioned how long I would live in a false reality without real growth.

I spoke to my own traumas as if it was a breakup. The love is lost. I know you want my love. As time goes on and you get to know me, you'll find it harder to be filled and obviously want more of me. I have more faces, more of me, to show you how much out of your league I am. To study me, is the only true thing left for you to feel like I'm in a moment with you.

I stared into your eyes and watched you live this moment, I saw you pour yourself into us as I grew further and further away. We both couldn't be this lost, so I made sure to overachieve in all the areas just to watch you enjoy yourself. Yet you had the nerve to question the extent of my love? Did you forget that I let the guilt go? The universe is tricky, putting such obstacles in my way with such precision to test me and see how much I really wanted to grow. Fate was going to do its bidding no matter what and I wanted to be here to watch it.

This transition Gordo led me on all came from a dream I had. The dream was a version of my death. I dreamt of getting the news that I had 2 days left of life and the feeling was so universal. I felt everything, deeply piercing my chest, collapsing my thoughts and just like that, I was stunned. It was good and bad, hot and cold. This left me empty to the extent I couldn't even process the emotions. Giving everything until there was nothing left.

My biggest fear was dying because I was always living. I said, "LIVING," not just breathing, and I was Great at living. The most confusing part of that dream is that before that version, only one other version existed. I had invested in my death for 20 years with the same thought of me dying in a vehicle and all of a sudden, I was given a heads up of 2 days?

This was the moment of change. I couldn't fear my death anymore when I had already created the thought of trusting God's will. I was always the driver, no matter how intoxicated I was. I would never hand over my keys, and I confess to the many nights I risked not only my life but also the lives of others. This wasn't right, but I knew my mother feared my mysterious life that

I left her out of so much that I counted on all her prayers to save us all.

I couldn't continue to put the burden of my decisions on my mother's prayers. I stopped driving, sitting in the backseat with a chauffeur was the life of a boss. Bullet proof with a sunroof so that I could enjoy my ride as I looked up to the sky with my own prayers of gratitude. I had to let go of the control, let someone else take over the wheel to truly enjoy this ride. This was the Cruise Life, and I respected that motion. I do this every day and then I wake up and do it all over again.

"PRAYER"

"Thank you, God, for picking me for this. Only you could create me with all this strength to withstand all the lies the world tells us. Nothing would be worth it without you. You never giving up on us deserves all the praise. I put myself through the unnecessary and wounded myself in ways only you could heal. Every beating was worth it in the end, just to see the smiles on everyone's faces. Nothing could stop us! I do this all for you, you have my soul."

I can't believe the time we tried to sell out. The pain was so unbearable that we almost quit on you. The darkness was swallowing us and I was so out of it that I couldn't even feel you. I'm so disgusted at the thought of such betrayal and here I am SHINING thanks to your will. You gave me the right to be the best and never will that put me anywhere near the purity I know you have for all of us. Nothing is the same without you. I just want to grow in this partnership to lead your kingdom to prosper and be victorious in your name.

I had to evolve from the chains my ancestors had been enslaved to for so many generations. I needed to become the man I always wanted my father to be for me. I knew he was hovering over me, keeping his weight on my shoulders as he had once done when he was alive. I could feel his energy still present, guiding me away from the mistakes that he made. I want to acquire a certain level of status where I can hold my composure and control all this energy to become a master of our failures.

So many changes had evolved within me, this was a choice. I had to choose a different path from the rest. I didn't do any of this to be better than anyone else, I did all of this so I wouldn't be treated like everyone else. It was either that or just living a revolving life. This was never a difficult decision for me.

I kept myself away from the masses to preserve the purity I had worked so hard for. To shut down all the things in this world that I didn't support or believe in. In all the changes, don't forget that I'm still unpredictable and myself. I had taught myself to be uncomfortable. I know how to make myself uncomfortable just to feel pressure so that true growth happens. You couldn't know my next move even if I told you what it was.

I'm now this rich man, who grew the same way that a sequoia grows in the Great Giant Forest. The sky is not a limit, but instead a vast space where I dictate the flow of the winds. Not because I command the winds to blow, but because I understand how the wind blows. I became one with life to provide life. My life is a metaphor, and it is your job to decipher it. In my story, the clues to a mindful existence can portray any person's basic needs. I create change, I am Great.

It was when all my staff thought that things were smooth that I was finally in a routine with no worries. I had even put all the bills on autopay along with my payroll and allowances I gave my loved ones. I wasn't going to let you forget about me, so I would wake up and make a drastic change, "Thank you for waiting on me, but today I'm going to walk."

In life, there are action periods and resting times. It was time to act now, so I lightened my feet and stopped walking so that I could run. As my thoughts flowed, I still couldn't understand how people could be so content with regular shit. How could you allow yourself to be so distracted away from the truth. Sports, shopping, clubs, social status, and jobs. This was all peasant level thinking, to be this poor in the mind when the riches of this world are all in creations and ideas, not the bait of the distractions.

I wanted the answers to be the help people needed to want. It was on this run that I met the answer I called for. Sometimes, people are in a place where even $100 on the floor has no value, and they are detached from a care in the world and do not even have a reason to spend. This was the answer to detach from the idea that $100 could be needed for anything, knowing all the spending in the world solved nothing and that the world was doing what it was meant to be doing. Don't be selfish, I told myself, it may not be doing nothing for you or me but on the other side, someone is being cared for in ways far more important than a dollar sign. Our true job is to be happy and that is all. Just LOVE to be happy.

Find purpose and that's how you find love. Love isn't something you wait for or find in another being. You have to become the love you want someone to give you. To start, love yourself, love yourself so much that it makes you want to share that love. Pick who to love and don't give your love, become the love that they see. This is how one needs to love, if not, you'll forever wait. Do this only if love is what you seek to gain in this life. I wanted to love everyone, so this, for me, wasn't enough.

The more and more "deeper" you build a bond or connection, the less and less the physical aspects of life matter. My journey didn't become any easier as I grew wiser, but I wouldn't say it ever got harder. With knowledge didn't necessarily come understanding, the skill that I acquired was accepting. We need to be aware that we aren't all at the same capacity and that nothing really has to make sense. For me, the difficult task was to contain my energy and put forth a form for mass production. Giving individuals my undivided attention was exhausting and the success turn around was unfruitful simply because emotions always get involved.

There wasn't enough time for sympathetic emotions, and I had no patience for incompetent mortals. I was blessed with the knowledge to serve the most high, so I couldn't fathom the journey amongst mesmerized degenerates. I questioned God over the motives for sending me back to these worlds and what was my goal? The lessons were obvious each and every time they arose, but I knew that wasn't my failure because I was well aware I would never stop learning.

The experience is not to "Know" but to still think deeper than what I know. Marinate on what I thought I knew by thinking of how that all made me feel. I needed to cure the numbness inside and still want, to still love. Attempt to bring back that faith of a child by getting to know Guero all over again. I was remembering how I came in naked, and just like clothes, I started adding it layer by layer like weights. Stress, problems, to-do's, goals, and expectations.

I was narrating my past, trying to catch up to my current moment. God was in full manifestation, the more I opened up with expressing myself, the more my soul was enriched. I saw the symbolic essence behind this journey just to remind me that we could plan but never control. That God does in his timing and that I was now enjoying the divine work for the very first time in my existence. To uncover the meaning of what it meant to be living in the past by being in the way of just being. Every now and then, I like to go back and see if I missed something, warping the time to slow down and see if I discover something new. The whole point was to tame your mind; it was never like me not wanting to know my own mind.

It wasn't my job to know your mind or judge your decisions. We can all seem ok but inside, it's not all the same. No one else could have done this. I was chosen to be the student of this silent chamber. I spent my time mastering the silence of the mind, the one people say works. Think, say and then do but this is no start or end. The mind is a place for the strong and the dead, wonderers of the unknown. Understanding this place is what gives control, how you pursue control is what determines the quality of the power you may obtain.

Power didn't matter to me that's why this task was gifted to me. The lost think that power leads to ultimate peace, how naive to assume such baffling ideas. This is the reason why I teach in the manner that I do. I show you the way just to leave you at the door because I'm merely a gate keeper who in the midst of seeking life, gave his soul to God for all eternity. I have no regrets; on the contrary, I stand as a giant all on my own, proud to be worthy of such responsibility.

I'm the tower at the gate watching your path in attempts to find the light at the end, and from here, I observe the many roads that many souls take and each time one finds the way, the skies illuminate in celebrations! This is me always searching for freedom, every evening praying for your healing. If you go through with the intention to get "stuff", "stuff" you will have. Think that if you do, it doesn't matter what gets done. If I really sat there and listened to everything I heard I would believe anything. Each and every time you said you quit and couldn't do it anymore would never have led to your success.

My life was on repeat, and if this was my life, it was good. I had what many wanted, I saw what many didn't look for, and I felt what many didn't know existed. Devouring life with no limit, boundless to any chackles, God knew I was at his service by choice. I was grateful for such freedom and honored at his command. God made sure I was never alone.

At the top of the tower, the infinite skies sent winds to keep me company, caressing my soul making sure to keep me warm through the lonely nights. I am happy to have this to share with you. Sometimes I get really sad because you have no idea, there's been so many people who claimed love for me before they even knew how to love themselves. I'm so much that I drain people and they can't keep up, and at this point, they figure the easiest thing to do is to give up. The true reward lies at the end of the tunnel, fighting an unknown battle that you're managing blindly, which is the most exciting part of this whole game.

You do understand that life is a game and that we are playing for our souls. Everything we do is a choice, and each choice has a unique outcome. Have you ever asked yourself why we are having this experience? I think we can agree that the ultimate goal is to detach from this life and find eternal peace. I don't believe people come forth with solutions because people want what they want but our wants aren't solutions. My job is to help everyone figure that out.

There are many worlds happening simultaneously, life is a complex playing field for all of us but you should only worry about how you lead your world. "Every little count" is a classic saying, imagine a glass sitting over a dispenser where a drop fills the cup. One drop at a time, eventually, the glass becomes full. Are you full? Being full is a measurable extent of any aspect or feature of something. Anything, a situation, problem, or an answer. God gave me the ability to fill souls in the hollow spaces of creation. I want to teach you how to live.

Dimensions make life more profound. We are an object to two worlds at once, flesh and spirt.

Flesh, is you "trying?" This refers to everything that gets in the way of just being. Spirit is our truest nature, that initial reaction that knows right and wrong without a question. Life isn't about feeling good, it's about the truth and our job is to find our way in the truth. The job isn't for anyone to "make" you play ball. I can throw the ball, but I can't force you to throw it back. I just want to see if you want to play catch with me.

Everyone thought that everything I am just happened overnight, as if I had a blueprint for the game of life. If you step out and go play, does this mean you're naturally good at playing? I wasn't one to get lost in a win or a loss; I never kept scoring because I just kept scoring. Know that I consistently fail just to understand my limitations, "Forbidding is forbidden to us." You should be able to tell when you're dialed in. Realize when you have wasted moves and teach yourself not to be a waste. Every move is to be done with instincts, this is true perfection.

I am not perfect; only God is, even amongst Giants, its God who leads. I understood that if God made us in his image this meant that I just had to do my best to be perfect. Honesty is true perfection. You can lie to anyone but never to yourself. Would you say this is proof that God is within? Proof is the evidence that establishes the truth of a statement. There's no such thing as a lie; a lie is simply denial disguised as a false statement. Sometimes, creating a lesser problem is better than proving a point to a bigger problem. It is a choice to let denial go.

I tamed all my defects and then concealed them. It would be extremely difficult for you to weaken my spirits. I was prepared to lose everything that I had worked for. None of this did I make nor invent, it was gifted to me for being loyal to a cause much bigger than myself. I just found all this along my journey, unwrapping itself like an onion. The layers of life made me realize what good was it to conquer so much of Earth and not be able to receive a small patch of heaven.

Time enlightened me where humans failed to do so. I needed to understand and not be waiting for people to understand me. I watched as others depleted in trying so hard to keep up, everyone was doing the same things. It was all a programming that everyone was accustomed to follow and think that this is what life was "supposed" to be like. There was so much more to life, and I'm here to tell the truth. I've drawn all these ideas and memories from my own experiences.

I enjoy doing homework, the late hours when the silence roams the air and makes my candles flicker. Reviewing my living moments over and over again just to know what it feels like at all ranges of emotions. I do things consciously, so every move has been planned to the very end. Without a plan, there is no connection. Without connection, you aren't truly living. I want to give you life by being an example of how you can find yourself. If you want to know how I move, let's start at the beginning of each day.

The lighting in my bathroom is red, that is the first room I step into when I begin my day. I brush my teeth and stare at the pigments that influence aggression and passion. I take control of my energy rooting myself with courage and stability. I shower and cleanse myself from the night wondering dreams that attempt to linger with sleep for a slow start. I won't allow it, I play motivating music with upbeats and get this vessel moving. Now, I'm in the groove as I dress myself for success. I do my absolute best each and every day to trick my ego into thinking it's being fed.

In all reality, I am the type to starve myself just to feel hunger. My own reflection couldn't keep up with me, let alone get ahead of me, I'm still unpredictable. It's not just about understanding, the heart has to agree with what the mind understands. If you can sit here and say that you agree, then the soul has begun to develop. This, too, is just the beginning for me, I had been stuck in the spirit realm, thinking my work was done but the plan was much bigger than I thought.

When we are born, the war begins. It's a constant battle of living life, and although we believe we are in control, we simply guide the path. The start and the end are as fragile as the bridge of time. In my war, I was willing to sacrifice good people for a greater good. That greater good was the sense of humanity. This wasn't my first lifetime, and I wasn't going to allow it to be our last. Have you ever heard how the oldest trees survived the most difficult situations?

For you, a difficult situation is like picking amongst the truth and denial. To choose your needs over your wants. What path is correct if it all leads to the same place, is it the class of that journey or your expectation for what you "deserve"? Can one truly designate what they deserve if they've yet to live the future, which is what shows the qualities considered to be worthy of. It was the manner in which I spoke of our differences that constantly challenged me to grow. I still had lessons to learn that I didn't even want to work for. I still considered myself to be an example of what one can become. I'm still not done.

Every moment was sculpting me, although it was a nuisance to endure growth and continue. It never ends, except now wasn't as before when I couldn't handle tension without snapping. I taught myself a new game, to make things a bit engrossing for the spectators. When life put me on the upside down, I understood it was just to play a different board, this made me have more substance. I laugh now as if I took two scoops of pre-workout, baby aspirin to thin out my blood flow to just go sit in a sauna for an hour and meditate. This is how I travel to other worlds beyond my naps, where peace lasts forever and all it took was to adapt to the temperature and control the heart trying to jump out of my chest.

When your heart is racing, it isn't what the doctor "say," it's truly just your body adjusting to new energy levels. Knowledge was more powerful than any medication. Medications were all my conquered demons. Everything I left behind me was unsavory, and the more I went on, the bigger destruction grew. I'm not being negative or overexaggerating; I just want others to know what I see coming before it comes. I get frustrated and think of helping but that isn't my job. I have to learn to stay detached because I'm still learning and growing myself.

I'm well aware that although they haven't had my experience in their own journey, just being here says they've been a long way. I know how to lead by reason and self-reflection. I don't help because it's God who helps. I serve so that I may navigate other realms because I know I can. Maximizing everything is a luxury, and living a life worthy is picking the most difficult levels. There are no regrets for my broken soul as payment in this game. This is what has come of my life and I'm always ready to gamble for the sake of growth.

The satisfaction I get each time I win is always worth the emotions I endure. Life isn't about the objects; it's more about what those objects represent. Victories stand for hardship, failures, work, and how many times I dragged myself back up to my feet. To pay for joy with my pain carried more value than pleasure. Pleasure is something we seek and continue to need more of, as pain is that piercing hold that remains and lasts forever.

Surviving everything just to know and share. A selfish victory would mean that I would feed off of the envy others may have. I feed off the thrill of living what others are scared to live. Even these things that seem to stem from negative ideas aren't a fit for me, so I convert them into outlets for others to see the possibilities. I want people to see how beautiful life can be if you live with intention and do things with a clean mind. A mind with no filter, a mind so spontaneous that you can't keep up.

None of this was ever truly for me, it was always for the people. The ones most lost with less to give because it meant nothing to serve those at the top or equal to me. Those under you deserve the most care because to be under means no one has ever cared for you before. To me, this matters, I am successful but I just can't let all this go. I can't just live a good life and not share for others to also do the same.

Even when I had nothing, I couldn't be comfortable. I always felt like I was a hit, and people would watch and conspire against me. I couldn't bare the idea of letting myself be a casualty to the lessons of life. Instead, I took the world in my hands and rolled it up into a ball, chewed it to pieces and swallowed it down like a snack. A snack was not worth the work, so I threw it all up, knowing from the beginning that I didn't even like this flavor. I would do things like this consciously and laugh as if I had wasted a perfect meal. It was cruel and disregarded all your feelings, all of my feelings.

What changed was that I finally decided to deal with all my feelings. I stopped ignoring all my problems and just decided to face the music. I fell deep into a blackhole, and it became soothing melodies of all the torn memories that I had once buried to disintegrate. The smaller you break down the pieces, the harder it'll be if you decide to put them together and understand them.

I want everyone to understand that I'm always sad, everything is broken for me. Living my life without my father here to impress, I had nothing to prove. No one mattered to Guero, the kid in me, because for him, everything was under his father's judgment. Your opinion of me is irrelevant and holds no value. Everything was felt with an aggressive depth. The pain lingered without reason, but I understood all that had no reason.

I found reason in the solace of an empty room. I couldn't say that I was that empty inside. I can't necessarily say that no one matters, because the father in me still thinks of his beautiful daughters to inspire. Pops thrives on the ideas to be a safe place for them to develop their potential. Geo thinks of the probability of getting himself together and making his family and friends proud. As I said before, "God is in every place and in everyone." Find the right place where you can be ok.

We are all on the spectrum. Something is always "wrong." Are you a lot miswired or just a lot? My dad always said that in this life to "make it," you had to be smart enough, or dumb enough. You couldn't be in between; being in the middle was as safe and mediocre as one could be. I knew I wasn't dumb enough, many said I was so smart, but I was really just so close for a very long time. I didn't give up, I worked when everyone slept and slept when I had no time to sleep.

I watched as others who did so well depleted but I gradually slid into character. While everyone around me fell off into the common population, I grew in solace. I wasn't alone, God was always with me, talking to my mind, keeping me sharp. I have a physical body, so I can't be in the world I belong, but I can take myself there just to touch it at any time. You call this meditation, I call this relationship. Right now, this is where I am and where I have to be just to hold myself together.

I still won't take your medication! When you're gone, it's all gone. How can you want to experience life if you can't hang on? It's a bit controversial because I'm over there, touching that life, but I'm here with you. It's like I don't want to leave; I just want to be selfish and continue experiencing. I found a skill that my father didn't, and that's why I survive. I discovered a way to take all of it with me—the other worlds I had been jumping to just to play. I bring everything back here to share with you.

I'm the library, the books you read when you close your eyes to sleep. I found the books hidden within my brain, and I took the time to read them. Learning without the influence of any drug was my greatest accomplishment. It was like overthrowing a whole government in a battle you were meant to lose. I want to teach people to be pure with all their failures—to have the guts to admit them and ask for forgiveness. Getting lost in the influence is like hiding, scrambling for shelter. The wind blows through all cracks, and being high was a crack in the shelter. How ironic that the government provides a shelter for those cracks in your soul.

To be high…

"I knew what it felt like to force myself to be calm and patient, claiming I was collected. Just a little hit to take all the problems away, and when that high went away, the problems just kept coming back. I just wanted to be at peace, so what was the true purpose to go back and come back to the same shit. Why do the same shit instead of elevating and seeking answers to those feelings that I ran from? I wanted to be high forever, for it not to go away. So, I did this shit sober, and I felt the pain and joy every fucking day."

The true level up came from taking myself to the same state of consciousness sober, and now I'm remarkably thorough. I destroyed everything that once was in me so that I could make the new room for the new story. This idea came from the belief that the world isn't prepared to destroy itself, and I felt it was my job to make sure it didn't do so. Many people have said this isn't even a good place to be and I'm truly sorry you've experienced it in that manner.

Emotions aren't a mistake, so how can we use them to elevate the perception of life? For starters, don't try to unlock new parts of the brain if you haven't taken the time to comprehend the ones formed as a child. Confront your traumas and find a way to forgive the damage. Write about it, talk to someone, get help or deal with it on your own. Don't take this onto new places and expect the world to adjust to your bullshit.

Remember, it is unjust to make our opinions facts in the worlds of others. Others who may never even have a similar comparison of their life to even understand the slightest possibilities of a world like yours to exist. "At the very end of the day, we are all alone," I told myself this many times in my pain. With the pressure of this being my reality, I decided to teach myself to do for people the things they couldn't do for me. I may not know you personally, but I know us. All the versions of myself that haunted my decisions.

This isn't a joke, but I do laugh at the idea that I'm a lunatic with multiple worlds where I play different characters just to see how it is to live another life. I did this all from watching others, I became so good at observing what the regulars do and mirroring it. This is exhausting because, as a physical form, we are on 24/7 and it's real work putting on my show.

Example

I've had a long, busy day of "work," and I get invited for drinks off the clock where I should be having fun mingling and I catch myself thinking that I'm networking. I'm making sure to form the correct facial expressions to the dialogue happening, laughing at shit I don't think is funny and forcing myself to recall some sports highlights that played in the background at some other "hangout." All this work just to stay connected and be ready to have some input. It never fails for someone to think I'm lost but I'll be ready to defend myself and throw them out of their own game. To think somehow, I manage such stress because of an articulate account of my own experiences is astonishing.

Could it be possible that in a world so vast as ours, I become enormous and make others feel small? I don't mean to do that; I just think of myself as being so big that others feel small. I could never take the blame. Nothing was ever my fault because that would mean that I was responsible for a misfortune in someone else's story. That doesn't even make sense because it's not even my story to cause an accident. You can call me single-minded and stubborn but don't forget to say I'm also obsessive.

I obsess over the growth and lessons we are to learn. I'm commanding in the orders to provide enough pressure for this growth. I believe that I am a self-righteous complacency and I say this to you in the most objective, respectful manner. Many thought that Geo didn't give a fuck and that he was selfish, well I swallowed him up and used his little input to become the fat rich old man that I am today. Gordo, a man who can't even handle the pleasant idea of throwing out his own trash. After all, he had been through why would he pleasantly throw out the trash?

I feel like I'm the gatekeeper for the dark side and the light side. I'm the only person willing to do the dirty work and go to the forbidden places to try and save people from their own demise. The pain that I inflict and witness is like shoes scraping on the streets, constant and endless. I taught myself the cold, careless ways of loving. A solace time to pick you up and let you fall. Could we agree that this is a beautiful surgical subtle gesture that requires precise handling. That loving is like licking the plate clean of crumbs.

How do we explain the way I feast on all that isn't physically visible? Like the tension, I feel when you begin to come around believing all my sweet nothings. It's a rush. I get to smell your scent traveling down the halls as anxiety rises when I hear your voice and think of how your sound waves navigate my mind. I'm crazy in love with all that allows it.

I'm twisted, so I scream to show how much I'm enjoying myself. To binge on such a meal and explode in fulfilling tenderness. I wanted the world to feel what I felt, to forget their ignorance and expect the sun to always shine. Many people are already living all this, but they just can't recognize it. They have a lens shielding them from reality and distracting them with a world of fairytales.

This is a nightmare and we are so selfish that we continue to come back and experience it just for a "good time." There is nothing here worth the pain we endure, so we must stop working for this measly dream and focus on the afterlife. Get right with God because it's only a matter of time before it's too late. Make sure that you can forgive yourself for your mistakes and reach your peace. Every me must find its place.

If we are all the same, I can't have an extension of me representing me the way you typical humans do. Let me take you to the forest to feed and recharge, offer you as my sacrifice to the land. I believe that I was meant to put you through hell for the simple selfish need to roll up the whole world. Does this then counter to make it a selfless act? Am I right or am I wrong to make these calls and assume you'll understand and be willing for the same cause as I?

If she said yes and turned off manage control, we could have some real fun. Experiencing all the interesting things that happen once one is aware. To distinguish the difference between what you actually and what your identity tells you to believe. I love you so much to sit back and watch you get lost in oblivion. We can't fix something that's fucked because it just gets worst. I had to keep it pure and be honest for things to be done right the first time. I'd be a fool to consider going back and making different decisions in time for the sake of trying for a better outcome, this would just make the timeline dig deeper, making this a deeper life problem.

I'm not perfect but I'm real. True to myself and true to you if you want me to. Can you cope and survive the excruciating pain of reality? How deep is the extent of your love if it's easier to quit than to pull? What lengths are you willing to fight for if your emotions get the best of you? Now, how worthy are we of an empire when the walls crash down with just a couple hits. This isn't rocket science, just the true nature of true love.

I will confess that such greatness isn't probable because to reach a higher plane of existence, we must become one aside from our independent existence. I have the idea to conquer gravitational power just to imprison the stars so that I may catch fire. I see myself gracefully walking in flames as if burning was non-existent. I am on fire and I will burn down into ashes at the sake of my hopes and dreams. I knew my actions would cost me my soul in exchange to indebt myself to the most high. I loved you so much I had to hide who I was becoming and let go of the grip I had on this mortal life. It was difficult to let you all go, I couldn't continue to protect you from the ugly truth.

The truth is that I used everyone for an experience. I made you all a part of my story, a sick, twisted fantasy that would develop into a lesson for everyone to learn from. You could use this and entertain your clouded sight with my imagination, or you could read between the lines and believe in the ability to invent such a critical broken heart. A soul that tortured itself in memories as it cornered itself in the darkest crevices to provoke fear and solitude. We learned to play with energy the same way that energy played with us. We took turns playing devil's advocate, conspiring on the world's twisted ways, getting even just to humble the balance of our hearts.

It sounds crazy to play on such a thin boundary of sin, knowing that sin is equal to spiritual death. I am crazy but no fear was instilled in me because I had already chosen to humiliate myself to my knees, begging for the presence of God. Many times, I hit rock bottom and never did I beg for mercy, instead I thanked God for teaching me with his ruling because I knew I was prepped for the battle. These moments are what made the difference between finding myself vs accepting myself.

How to find one that isn't lost? The only loss we can take is giving away our soul to devious thoughts, knowing that is the absence of God. I'm now ascending into a place where I can see the world, I just can't touch it. As my life became richer so did my heart, the abundance of knowledge flowed through me to get to you.

It cost me everything. I quit on everyone. I couldn't accept the level of human life that you all provided me with, it was weak. So I got tired and sent everyone away push after push. I'd leave my meditative state and work in your world just to watch you all bullshit around. It was tormenting for me to see everything you lacked that made you feel less than what I saw in you. You blamed me for the simple fact that I cared more than you to understand.

I thought that if you watched me work you would follow and mimic my ways into creating your own style. I made a quick decision because I knew the first thoughts are your natural pure ideas, anything that second guessed was tainted. To witness you so unsure created doubt. I'm sorry, I don't trust anyone, nor do I believe anyone cares for me more than I for myself. It's difficult to give away my space where I stand on my own two feet just so you could take a look at what I see. I questioned why you were so stuck, I was able to attend your church but you couldn't even find mine. I know you and I'll always be able to find you.

Chapter Nine:
I'm not a Giant, I'm a God

I was glitching, trying to override everything that I was programmed to react to. The system didn't like the part of me becoming bigger than all of this. Knowledge had poisoned my beliefs and now I had no limits. I took the restraints off that kept me distracted with the masses when all that truly mattered was me. The selfish course that I was on is creating greatness and the world wasn't prepared. A world who I gave no option to and at the snap of my fingers, learned to submit. Everyone watched me work tirelessly, thinking I'd collapse, unaware that inside of me lived a fat, rich old man who needed to be fed.

I want to be clear that this is not some religious guide, but the truth is that I couldn't defy a relationship that made me complete. Never can I be an influence that doesn't allow free will; choices are yours and infinite. I'm simply committed to my selfless devotion to serve the God of all Gods. You can't find my God in a book nor in a temple. Let's be clear: this isn't an attack against any entity that guides you on a positive path.

Give me a chance to explain myself, if you can step outside yourself and have a healthy open mind to see if we are on the same page but just took a different path to get there. I believe that the entire creation is God and that it's God who gives because it all belongs to God. With that being said, God is that last piece of energy that makes us complete. This is found within yourself when you're able to get past all doubts and trust your true instinct. You can spend your whole life lying but deep inside, you always know when you're wrong. Any choice you make tells you if it's correct before you make it.

I've done everything, gone down your road, checking every detail thoroughly just to tell you this story. Innumerable times I watched myself consciously in absurd places.

ME: "When the fuck is it going to be enough, I might not even make it out of this one this time. I know better, I'm too smart!"

VS

US:" You're only this smart because you continue to chase experiences. I'm not making excuses, how else would you tell this magnificent story?!"

You have no idea what psychology I played. I took a lot of losses separating myself from the rest, a constant war getting bombarded in persistent criticism. It was a spiritual challenge that I was determined to win.

My biggest weakness was always the flesh, all the regular shit we are programmed to submit to. Luxuries, sex, drugs, all the temporary fun and it took a great deal of discipline to expunge. I don't judge anyone because I believe in a truth that allows failures and weakness. I proved this fantasy to be dead in its own existence by watching the cycle repeat itself.

Perfect example: You go to work and exhaust yourself in a schedule of tasks "have to's." You get paid as a distraction from the idea that you earned something in exchange. The weekend is free to do as you please and because you deserve it, you'll squander all that you spent just to run dry and do it again.

The purpose of LIFE is to be ALIVE. It's a condition that distinguishes us with the capacity for growth with a constant change of existence. Why would you jump in a hamster wheel looking forward but remain stagnant? We are creators with the power to paint our own image of what we want to see. I have an eye for the little things that make up the entire thing.

I am a remover of obstacles, the true embodiment of all aromas of love, a timeless essence of answers and the strength to carry you when you are weak. You have me within yourself when nothing gives and, in this quest, I believe you have all that you need because I gave you everything. What I don't believe is that I can absolutely hand you freedom and true salvation. In this world, you get what you hunt. It's up to you if you stay lost in starvation, constantly needing to fill or find a path that fulfills your purpose of helping and doing your part. This is all about what you can do for us.

What I do for us, I would kill myself for you just to make you feel loved. I would jump into your world, your fraction on your timeline and find perfection. We are perfect in each existence! Thank you for being you, always you that I know with all its perfect imperfections. As the landscape changes from place to place, as beauty molds to the climates provided in natural actuality. I pay to live like this, to live a different me and play a whole new role each and every day.

I left the coded autopilot mind with the boring script and predictable experience. That place lost me in translations where I was unentertained by you. In this dialogue, I was a lie, a fraudulent version of mass production. Incapable of true love, with nothing to give and just pain to take. The memories of those times are vague and inaccurate in terms of the valuable purpose of our magical soul. Filled with desires of that flesh yearning thirst until I tasted something more adequate for my quenching pallet.

Sweat and tears weren't enough, I wanted blood. With the blood, I took intuition, sacrificing all power as a sign of the fact that you belonged to me. I kept this dear to me, and never burned it just to prove a point. I'm going to confess a detestable moment in my past, one that is cursed for life with no possibility of reason. You may question the nature of how I love to love and how it torments the hearts of those that fell. This is actually my favorite story because I was at my weakest place, vulnerable with no chance to win. I was being toyed with like a child and it made me not care to take everyone else down with me.

A plan to show the whole world that this life had no purpose and how much it didn't matter. I was convinced of my next life and completely done with this one. I was to be martyred in my faith and the storm was brewing; slowly, my thoughts boiled with no time to simmer. The thunder roared in anger and my spirit wept like a scared child. The end was coming and I wasn't going to end my story in disappointment. I was selling my soul and predating my destiny. Can't say I was thinking straight amongst the drugs and alcohol I immersed my judgement in.

I want to say that it was all the losses I had taken, including my dear father's death. That would be a lie, all just excuses to derail my life into a meaningless empty vessel. Making hard choices is exactly that: hard. A great deal of force for the lessons to be learned was needed to reach my highest human potential. What was more difficult was for me to witness the repercussions of my own actions. In the life of a human's experience it's crucial to have purpose, and preferably for it to create a positive outlet. If you are to endure all this pain, make the ending beautiful. Let the results of your sacrifice make an impact for a greater future. I didn't understand this yet.

She lay on my bed with her caramelized skin, tummy down and everything else went up in the air. It was a heaven-sent view of the hell I was in. I sat in the corner, journaling my thoughts with tears smearing down my skull. She knew I wasn't ok and knew exactly how to distract me, "Hey Geo, you know I LOVE YOU, right." I saw right through her, dazed in my emptiness. At this moment, I had the Great thought that changed my life path, "You really love me?" She replied, "I'd do anything for you," smiling with all the lies in her mouth. She was a fucken demon.

How do you smile at someone who's on the edge of ending their own life? I was lost but I wasn't fucken stupid. I was blind by the sweet moans you pushed when I railed my cock in your guts just to feed my flesh with the flow of water that rushed out onto my pelvic area and down between our legs. I can't forget the thrill of the power I recalled while gagging you in your own creamed underwear. It's disgusting but this was the specific hell where my demons were able to dance. You gasped for oxygen, laid out exhausted, catching back up to the timeline and I went back to my table to write all my thoughts. I was conscious and aware, so I stared at you as I wrote. I wanted to be sure that my writing had power.

You smiled again, so I brought back the subject. Baiting you to reverse the clock to my lifeline I asked, "Would you really do anything for me?". You looked confused but you couldn't back pedal in fear I would unveil your true intentions. You were guarding me from changing my mind and living to fight another day. So, I read to you what I wrote to make you believe you had me fooled. I needed to empower you in order to convince you that you still had me tangled in your shadows.

WRITING

"Uneasy, a tincture of pheromones gale into me, wavering the vibrations invisibly tempting. Premeditating the epic outburst to a tender idea, I resisted. Pulling away in regret, things were perfect, her tranquility was worth it. Drifting around my room floated all her dreams and my worst nightmares, enjoying the clips revealing "

"Anything? Sign this in blood to show you're real". I held an ancient knife that was taken from a collector's display on one of my missions. Unsure what kind of energy the knife stored, you still didn't hesitate to cut yourself. As we watched the drops land on the paper, you balled your fist in pressure. You smiled and said, "ok, now you have to burn it and seal our deal," so I countered, "You burn it since it's your deal." Confused at my response, you couldn't even touch the paper. I tried handing it over and you moved away in fear. I kept trying and I saw the rage build up each time I started you to take it. I had you trapped, and it enraged you to have been played like the fool you are.

The fucken shadows belong to me! It was never the physical choking that did anything for me. It was when I saw the full submission. The power grew when I saw past your eyes how you completely folded. Giving yourself away by literally allowing me to strangle you as I took the life away from you. Taking the oxygen that kept you breathing and alive, this is how I stole from you without you knowing that I knew you really didn't care. You didn't care for anything other than letting me take it, luring me to believe that this was a purpose. The reality is that we are here to give and not to take.

You stormed out, upset that I wouldn't burn the paper as a contract. The lights flickered as I followed you to stay. The walls scratched in desperation down the halls, although it made no sense to be angry at a meaningless exchange. That's when I realized this was all real. I wasn't just high. I was playing with the devil the whole time. You gave me one last kiss before leaving, a trick to tickle the mind. I was scared to go back by myself. The house was eerie, and no one answered my calls to accompany me inside. Now, I needed solace for my soul, alone once again.

I learned a lot from this experience, this needed to happen. I'm not ashamed to speak on the length to which life dragged me. This is just an example of how twisted life can be, how naive we are allowed to be. Everything can be forgiven as long as change can redirect you. I told myself that everything would be used to inspire others for a change. They say don't change what isn't broken, but I say enhance what you consider golden.

We must starve before eating, if the intestines aren't emptied, we just poison ourselves. I committed to fasting to refrain from any such degenerative actions. This was difficult to see the beauty sucked out and plainly look at the soul I had to offer. Life had been sucked out of me and I had a ton of rebuilding to do. This didn't mean that I would never punish another soul, because it was my place to teach lessons and cause growth to trigger. I've always loved so much that I feel the need to hide the ugly truth of who I am.

I'm having this conversation with you to continue to develop my self-growth. In discussing, we may uncover understanding. It's like creating the outline of a picture you may someday get to color. My craziest dream was creating you. I saw myself in a workshop stamping your lashes on your wondering eyes. They sparkled as I held your hands while forming your frame with my tongue. It's a real work of art to create true love.

I'd like to say I know about love but when I sit back and think on the topic, I really don't know shit. I love to love and always give my all, but this always results to shit. I make a pretty mess and ache for not making things work out. I just leave all the parts of me behind as a trail paved in case I make it back. I need to get my mind right to be myself and succeed.

When you do things in the right state of mind, you can be as sick as you want because you can just go right back to normal. No harm, no foul, just the little twisted game I play whenever I'm healthy. It's the fasting that got me healthy but the game that derailed me. Life is weird like that sometimes. A test of our judgement and how we manage temptation. It was just so satisfying how my games acquired true love from them, all of them drawn like the ocean waves pull at your feet.

Laughing at demons as they hid when I welcomed them. No one wants to be exposed, but I took the stories you shy away from and spoke about them out loud. I went from battlefield to battlefield to find new struggles to feed the war I carried inside. This was ongoing and I knew it would never end, so I never would carry a watch when time for me was this irrelevant. I was stuck in the place of thinking, and if I didn't continue searching for answers, I would die inside. My own life had no value for me, my life was meant for all of you.

I wanted all the love to be gentle with me, for love to move with grace, especially when we were under fire. To manage things correctly and not allow me to be impulsive and inconsistent. I understood that love is the one thing that goes beyond death, which is why it triumphs in victory. I loved when a person carried themselves in exclusivity, to be limited in presence and discouraged by the chase. You have to be smart for those choices, and with someone smart is the only way to elevate. Only with these standards would I enjoy the victory.

For me, everything is easy because I know, I see and I understand. My love is like a warm bed, the feeling of ending a cold shower and going straight under the blankets. The way I hug you into comfort and bring you the relief of a safe place. A place of shelter from all the destruction and uncertainty. I watch you and see all that you're capable of, not sure if this makes you nervous but I'm just here to see you, dissect and digest. Everything else is a bonus for me. It was the world entirely I was after not a single human alone could fulfill me.

I had to make the world my bitch. The vision I had for this was everything. I was cumming and she was taking my soul. It was the first time I experienced this. I had torn down so many countless moments to now 30 years later, it is the first time for something like this. I pumped load after load of my efforts as she crawled her way up and down my skin. Breathing heavily as she approached me face to face, knowing I had my final breath suspended as, I enjoyed the ending. A final exhale before I saw my demise. I let go of my last breath and by the time I realized it was too late to take it back, our lips were already together as she sucked in every bit of oxygen out of my lungs, I was helpless. I gradually saw my aura be devoured so effortlessly.

This is the story of how we became one and I ended up as a gatekeeper to her world. I was a God created in this image. Crazier than anyone I ever came across for all the work I put into life. Regular humans get tired of suffering and become so ignorant that they look for something nonexistent, I never did. I wanted to learn about this, so I took it all in and became immortal.

From my past life, I learned that I had very low expectations but very high standards. I was capable of love, but it wasn't enough to work. When I realized that I was truly infinite and would never stop giving, it was part of that ending. I knew that the false expectation of a regular human would plateau in the fantasy life and stop giving me anything back.

I became disappointed that my true destiny was that of a God in love where he doesn't belong. In this place, my kind really wasn't welcomed, we were allowed to wander in fear of our power. We made others feel small because we had no fear of making mistakes. I saw the empty space you wanted to occupy. I couldn't lose the ability to understand what I had already started, none of this was for me because it was all for you. I wasn't just some self-important individual. The reality is that I am extremely important to a cosmic cause.

Belonging to a haven for brilliant minds, knowing that what I had brewing inside was worthy of forgiveness. Was it ignorant to think it was all great enough to make up for a lot more than it should? That all the sacrifices and careless actions bared no guilt? My genius didn't guarantee any wisdom, yet it brought me here. It took me far beyond this world of living, and I had a high price to pay. To assume people could even praise and honor so much pain that people were truly distracted while keeping up high the agony of war?

The Great War I battled continuously, the fight everyone likes to ignore and shut out. I was engaged in understanding far beyond theory. How could I dream of you, fantasize about the existence in my heart, but honestly, I couldn't love you the way you wanted me to? To offer a fight as a future, to promise and look after yourself in care, and to expect you to be content. Why couldn't this be enough? Greed is an evil infection, killing all possibility of a living affection. Gravity swallows the light like a black hole, keeping you stuck to the ground as you root yourself to the ideology of flesh. The politics of what is "right," trying to keep all my power in the shadows!

To never allow suppression of The Great Almighty. I wasn't just self-important, but the true nature is that we each are very important with the individual purpose to manifest the purest form of our capabilities. God didn't gamble, impeccable in all perfection of creation. So, I watched and waited patiently because only good could come from this. Temptation failed repeatedly due to frustration, to my understanding. I witnessed how my light grew brighter as I isolated myself, calling us the student of free will.

I have many memories of me tangled in my thoughts and interrupted in my peace. I always knew that soon enough, I would calm and settle into my being as if nothing had disturbed me at all. To make decisions that promote good and without a doubt. You had to be real to connect with me, honest with your thoughts, true to your words, and concrete in your actions. I had everyone convinced that I was crazier than I really could be.

My name is Zeta. Life is simple, and I'm a simple being.

Book Letter

Nothing is done alone.

The connection; this is to all the people who thought they weren't noticed. I was never alone, and it was thanks to all of you that this was possible. I went through so many emotions to build my memories. I'm here embracing the current, assuming all responsibility for my past. I don't expect anyone to agree with my life decisions, but I was polished by the friction.

To share my story, the life I created that became part of all my growth. To be accepted is how I define true love. Forever isn't the representation of something that doesn't end. This simply means it will be everlasting in the future. In relation to memories, we get to keep them. Good or bad, our creations belong to us FOREVER.

Let's accept the celestial work that allowed us to intercept. We need to be grateful that we are who we are for one another and that the universe came to meet us in unison. That the life lessons we cope with should never be undermined but instead accepted. For each individual only knows what makes them valid. Let's be gentle in our understanding and patient of the development.

This is what I think when I envision my life with my divine counterpart 👫 therefore, I believe in living to the fullest with the ones you love, being crazy by exploring and experiencing beauty all around the world. It's when we think we've found all we need that we find new ways to have more beautiful moments. One day we shall be older… we can sit on our death bed surrounded by all our kids and their kids to share our legacy and let them know…

NO ONE OUTLIVED US

Most importantly, we were given freedom together and on our own. This is an intro to the Mes. I want to share them individually and unpack the lore that they acquired. To give you permission and allow you to gaze at my truth for what it is. Everyone thought I was crazy and that I was losing it. And honestly, I did but I had faith that, in the end, I would get myself together to live and tell the story.

My love and devotion have been given to the existence of being an example of all living forms. I allowed self-sabotage to see what the lowest points of living may be like and how one could find the light at the end. Although I am sure many have endured much worse than I ever did, I was taught to understand understanding and to leave myself out of the experience. I feel for you the way God must have felt for me.

Everything was done to my design and manifested to please the ONE true God. I want to thank GOD, all the Glory is for his doing and work. The perfection that has been proved to me countless times, I won't ever deny or defy. I can't stress enough the worth of finding oneself in the will of GOD.

This book presents the truth about WHO I AM. I am the voice of vulnerability.

INSTRUCTED BY: GOD

MANIFESTED BY: US

ILLISTRATED BY: DRU

www.ingramcontent.com/pod-product-compliance
Lightning Source LLC
LaVergne TN
LVHW022013060526
838201LV00034B/342/J